"Something wrong?" said Gideon.

He tipped his dark head and lifted his hand as if to touch her, but obviously thought better of it because he dropped it slowly back to his side.

She wouldn't allow this to happen. She wished Gideon would stop looking at her, smiling at her. She wished he were a million miles away, wished she'd never taken this commisssion in the first place.

DIANA HAMILTON is a true romantic and fell in love with her husband at first sight. They still live in the fairy-tale Tudor house where they raised their three children. Now the idyll is shared with eight rescued cats and a puppy. But despite an often chaotic lifestyle, ever since she learned to read and write Diana has had her nose in a book—either reading or writing one—and plans to go on doing just that for a very long time to come.

WEDDING DAZE

DIANA HAMILTON

THE MARRIAGE QUEST

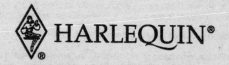

HARLEQUIN®

TORONTO • NEW YORK • LONDON
AMSTERDAM • PARIS • SYDNEY • HAMBURG
STOCKHOLM • ATHENS • TOKYO • MILAN • MADRID
PRAGUE • WARSAW • BUDAPEST • AUCKLAND

ISBN 0-373-80627-2

WEDDING DAZE

First North American Publication 2001.

www.eHarlequin.com

Printed in U.S.A.

CHAPTER ONE

'CAN I help you, love?'

Alice dragged her eyes from the white-stuccoed façade of the enormous, sprawling house and fastened them on the approach of a voluptuous, leggy blonde. She blinked. The sunlight was dazzling and so was the blonde.

Gathering herself, she opened the door of her immaculately kept small car and planted her sensibly shod feet on the raked gravel semicircle that fronted the building.

During the course of her work she had stayed in some fabulous homes, but for sheer elegance and style Rymer Court was out on its own. The best yet.

And immediately and predictably Alice felt at an enormous disadvantage. It had nothing whatever to do with the house, and everything to do with the incredibly sexy blonde. She towered a good six inches above her own insignificant five feet three and displayed her spectacular endowments to stunning advantage in a pair of minute grass-stained white shorts and a bikini top so tiny it boggled the mind.

Pushing her dark-rimmed owly glasses back up her short nose, she managed, 'Alice Rampton from Hearts and Flowers. I am expected.' She extended her hand and wondered if the knock-out blonde was the bride-to-be.

Almost certainly so. Hadn't her own assistant,

Rachel, gushed, 'With those looks and all that lovely money he could have his pick of the most gorgeous women in the world! He could have me at the flick of an eyelash. So whoever he's marrying has just got to be a knock-out. Some women have all the luck.'

That had been back at her Mayfair office, just after his initial appointment.

And Alice, too, had been impressed. Oh, not by his spectacularly gorgeous looks or the relaxed and lazy smile that seemed to imply that the recipient had miraculously earned herself a special and inviolable place in his affections. Unlike Rachel, she was above all that sort of stuff. No, it was his total lack of dither that had impressed her deeply.

In her by now considerable experience, the people who paid her to take charge of their wedding arrangements never knew quite what they wanted, oscillating between this, that and the other until she was forced to bite her tongue, close her eyes and devoutly pray for the patience of a saint.

But there had been none of that with Gideon Rymer. 'The wedding will take place from my home, Rymer Court,' he had told her in that warm, almost gravelly voice, and his presence on the opposite side of the desk had seemed to make her attractive office strangely airless and cramped. 'The reception is to be held in a marquee on one of the lawns, but apart from that everything else will be entirely in your capable hands. I expect you'll need to liaise with Janet, my fiancée. She and her mother, Gwen, are both with me at Rymer, so you will meet with them there. But they won't interfere, I promise you. As the professional at the circus you will have a completely free hand.'

He had sounded laid-back to the point of boredom, almost, and 'circus' was surely an odd way to describe his coming nuptials. His fiancée would surely have something to say about his promise of non-interference. She would have her own ideas about the way her day of days was to be organised, naturally.

He hadn't blinked at her standard charges, either, and that had earned her further approval. She gave excellent, faultless service—it was a matter of pride with her—and naturally charged accordingly. Some of her clients seemed unable to make the connection and haggled, which she disliked intensely.

But Gideon Rymer, at thirty-five the most successful young barrister around, handsome and breathlessly wealthy, was obviously sensible enough to realise that you only got what you paid for. He would want his wedding day to be perfect and she, the one-man band, was here to see that he got it.

'You must be Janet.' Alice hauled herself out of her brown study, uncomfortably aware that the sexy blonde vision was looking at her as if she'd lost her senses, no doubt wondering if she'd suddenly been struck dumb.

'Nah!' The cockney accent could have been cut with a knife. 'I'm Tossie, the gardener. Gideon said to keep a look-out for you. I'll help you with your bags to the house, shall I?'

Tossie's grin was infectious, and she tossed her head, sending pale, shoulder-length hair flying. Alice knew that if she released her own hair from its habitual braid—which she had no intention of doing—she could give the other girl a run for her money, in length, colour and sheer luxuriance.

At that totally unexpected thought Alice frowned behind her owly glasses. What on earth had come over her? She wasn't here to compete in the looks department. How could she, even if she wanted to, when she knew from her own looking glass, not to mention her elegant mother and her three gorgeous sisters, that she was a complete non-starter in that area?

She was here to do a job. A highly lucrative job. 'Thank you.' She smiled politely. 'That would be kind.'

Gardener? she queried inside her head. With looks like that she would have thought Tossie would be more at home on a catwalk or film set than grubbing around in the soil.

'I'll hand you over to Donatella—Gideon's house-keeper.' The object of her silent amazement broke into her musings. 'She's half-Italian and ever so nice. She'll show you your room and fix you up with coffee.'

Tossie's endless, gorgeous legs—finished off, Alice could now see, with lightweight canvas boots—were now loping elegantly across the gravelled sweep. She was carrying the single suitcase. Alice, feeling insignificant, brought up the rear with her briefcase in one hand and her capacious black leather handbag dangling from the other.

'Don't you think I should introduce myself to—?' She searched her memory banks for Gideon Rymer's fiancée's surname with difficulty. For some professionally inexcusable reason only his name had stuck. Then thankfully she found it. 'To Miss Cresswell first?'

'Nah.' Tossie's big blue eyes twinkled at her over a tanned, naked shoulder. 'Jan and her mum are over at the Manor House—the family home. They've moved in here while it's being done up. And about time too—the place was in a dreadful state. The Cresswell family's been there for centuries and I don't think anyone's given it so much as a lick of paint for the last fifty years. But they'll be back in time for dinner.'

Trailing behind Tossie as they skirted the elegant property, Alice tutted under her breath. She had expressly stated that she would arrive in Berkshire before lunch for her first consultation with the bride-to-be. And so she had arrived, all hyped up and ready to go, apparently to be left kicking her heels for the rest of the day when she could have been usefully employed back at the office.

Didn't Janet Cresswell realise what a rush it was all going to be? The wedding was to take place towards the end of June. It was now mid-May. Which left hardly any time at all to get everything done. All the marquee firms she usually dealt with could be fully booked...

'Dona—you in there?' Tossie poked her bright tousled head round an open side door.

Alice, feeling the midday sun—which seemed more concentrated in the cobbled inner courtyard— burn through the fabric of her neat grey suit, glowered at the frothy, fragrant displays of colourful annuals which burgeoned from dozens of terracotta containers and cascaded from a multitude of hanging baskets.

Was there no one around possessed of a sense of

urgency? Was everyone as laid-back and relaxed as Gideon Rymer had seemed to be?

His relaxed insouciance had particularly struck her at the time of their consultation. Perplexed her, too. She would have expected a top barrister—and one, so her subsequent researches had revealed, tipped to be amongst the youngest judges ever—to be sharp, incisive and impatient of time-wasters.

Somewhere a dove called, softly breaking the gentle, slow silence. Alice sighed with repressed impatience.

Maybe the housekeeper—when she finally put in an appearance—would be more on the ball. She certainly hoped so! And perhaps she could be persuaded to show her around, suggest which rooms the wedding guests could use as cloakrooms and rest-rooms. That would be a start of sorts.

Eventually, from the depths of the house came a languid, barely audible reply, and Alice's heart sank. No crisp on-the-ballness there, by the sound of it.

'I got Miss Rampton here,' Tossie yelled back. She set the suitcase down and turned on her effortless, wide white smile. 'She'll be with you in a tick. I'd take you through meself, only I've got mulch on me boots. Better get back to it, I suppose. See you.'

She loped away, her curvy backside wiggling provocatively, making Alice wonder if Tossie had been employed for her horticultural genius or something else entirely.

Which was none of her business.

Resignedly deciding that the half-Italian housekeeper had to be pitifully ancient and decrepit if it took her this long to respond to a summons, Alice transferred her handbag to her briefcase hand, picked up the suitcase and marched in through the door.

The corridor looked endless, with a bewildering number of natural oak doors let into the pale magnolia walls. But before she could decide which one to open first the one at the far end was flung open and a small, fiery whirlwind swept down on her.

'Oh! I'm sorry I've kept you waiting! I was whisking eggs for the zabaglione and didn't dare leave it. Here—' a pretty hand reached for the suitcase '—let me take that. I'll show you to your room. But how about a coffee first? Yes?'

Alice's grey eyes were huge. She blinked. If anything, this pocket Venus was even more sensational to look at than Tossie! The brevity of the black mini-skirt she was wearing with a sheer white voile sleeveless blouse was unlike any respectable working outfit she had ever come across.

'You—you're Mr Rymer's housekeeper?' she croaked. Alice watched the thickly lashed, big brown eyes go dreamy as a sensual little smile curved the rosy mouth.

'Yes. Lucky me! He's wonderful, isn't he? I love to cook for him, make everything here beautiful for him. I adore my job!'

'I can imagine,' Alice said repressively, then immediately regretted it. None of this—whatever 'this' was—was anything to do with her. If he liked to surround himself with adoring females then that was his business, and Miss Cresswell's, not hers. 'I'll skip coffee, thanks,' she added more mildly. 'I'd like to freshen up first.'

And then take a look around the premises, she

thought to herself, and decide which of the lawns Gideon Rymer had mentioned would be best suited for the marquee—provided she could get one at this late stage. And see which of the rooms would best lend themselves to cloakroom and rest-room duty.

'Fine. I'll show you up, then.' Donatella dimpled, twirling round, sending her long, silky black hair flying around her lovely face. 'You're going to be with us for—what? Ten days? Two weeks?'

They crossed the gleaming farmhouse-style kitchen at a trot, and beyond the baize door Alice watched Donatella's high heels twinkle across the richly shining parquet of the main hall and puffed, 'Goodness, not that long! Three days at the very most.'

As if she had nothing better to do than idle around for a couple of weeks when everything could be sorted, given some co-operation, in a couple of days!

'Oh.' The housekeeper paused, one hand on the ornately carved rail of the wide staircase that curved so elegantly upwards. 'Gideon said he expected—'

'Only two or three days.' Alice had got her breath back now and was able to restate her position very decisively. Never mind what Gideon Rymer 'expected', some people had to cram as much as humanly possible into the working week.

Sure, he would be writing the cheque to cover her hefty fee, but he was paying for what she could do, her organising abilities, not buying a great chunk of her time. Time was a precious commodity; she didn't believe in wasting it.

From then on she gave her attention to her surroundings: the richness of the carpets beneath her feet, the exquisite silk wall hangings, the great bowls of flowers that seemed to be everywhere, scenting the air and adding splashes of colour and light and texture, contrasting delightfully with the more sombre aspects—the heavy, gilt-framed portraits and perfectly proportioned pieces of probably priceless antique furniture.

And there were flowers in the room Donatella left her in too. A Chinese bowl of huge wine-red peonies on the gleaming surface of a rosewood table set beneath one of the three tall windows and a smaller arrangement of early rosebuds on the nightstand at one side of the big brass bed.

Whatever else, Gideon Rymer certainly had excellent taste. She was literally surrounded by perfection. She wondered whether she should envy his bride-to-be and decided not to.

At the moment, for economical reasons, she inhabited an austere bedsit near Euston station. She preferred to plough her profits back into her business and to splash out on the exorbitant rent of her Mayfair premises, because in order to attract wealthy clients she had to put on a successful front.

But she had recently started her own 'Get-Yourself-A-Decent-Pad Fund', and she would eventually, if her business continued to prosper, be able to provide herself with the type of home she wanted by her own efforts. Which was a darn sight more ethical than marrying some guy to get it, as her sisters had all done!

Catching a glimpse of her ferocious expression in the full-length pier glass, Alice pulled herself together. No good getting all uptight and tense about things. Her sisters had been blessed with fabulous looks and oodles of charm, but she, the plain runt of the litter—as she had once, to her mortification, over-heard her great-aunt Chloe describe her—had been born with ambition, determination and guts. Which surely had to be better.

Firstly, and most importantly, she unpacked the vast contents of her bulging briefcase and laid them neatly on the rosewood table, moving the bowl of peonies briskly aside, then straightened sharply as she heard the bedroom door open, the rattle of china.

As she'd left Donatella had murmured something about bringing up a tray of coffee, and, truth to tell, she could do with a cup now. She could drink it while she did the rest of her unpacking.

She swung round on her heels, the smile she had ready sagging away, leaving her staring open-mouthed. Gideon Rymer was carrying the tray in his long, strong hands. She hadn't expected him to be here at all, but to be safely away in his chambers or lazily, in that hopelessly relaxed way of his, defend-ing some luckless alleged criminal in the law courts.

And why 'safely'? she snapped crossly at herself inside her head. She was in no danger whatsoever from him. How could she be? The very idea was un-worthy of her, patently absurd.

'Coffee. How nice,' she croaked, her mouth sud-denly dry. When he had come to consult her he had been wearing a dark business suit, a crisp white shirt with a very faint grey stripe and a blue silk tie that had exactly matched the extraordinary colour of his eyes.

Now he was dressed in narrow-fitting stone-coloured denims topped by a body-hugging black sleeveless T-shirt, the casual outfit serving to under-line that the magnificent physique Rachel had raved about had nothing to do with the art of a clever, ex-pensive tailor.

'Dona said she thought you'd like some. And I thought it a good opportunity to renew our acquain-tance.' He put the tray on the low oak linen chest that footed the end of the opulent brass bed. There were two cups, Alice noted, a line of perspiration suddenly breaking out on her short upper lip. For some un-known reason he had a very odd effect on her.

She didn't feel intimidated. Not exactly. But swamped.

'Cream?' he asked with an upward sweep of one expressive black brow. 'Sugar?'

'Just as it comes.' Her voice didn't sound at all like her own and her hand had gone up, darn it, worrying at the corner of her mouth. It was a habit she'd kicked with no effort at all just as soon as she'd struck out on her own, got herself out of the confidence-sapping orbit of her exquisite mother and three gorgeous sis-ters.

She snapped her hand sharply down in time to re-ceive the cup he held out to her. She met his eyes and wished she hadn't, because they were the most breathtaking blue she had ever seen, even more thickly fringed with lashes as dark as his slightly rum-pled hair than she remembered. Smiling eyes, warm eyes, enfolding her, drawing her to him...

Literally fighting for breath, she took the cup and walked over to one of the tall windows, just to put space between them, and hoped, quite desperately, that he wouldn't follow. But he did, and she blurted, for something to say, 'You have a lovely home,' and knew, drainingly, how mousy she must look—especially when compared with the incomparable Tossie and Donatella.

'I think so,' he told her, his voice making her skin feel as if it had been rubbed with warm velvet. 'My paternal grandfather had it built on his marriage, around 1920. The family have been here ever since, and when my father died six months ago I decided to make it my base and give up my bachelor service flat in one of the new Docklands developments. It means more travelling, of course, but so far I haven't regretted it.'

Alice welcomed his snippets of personal information. Not because she wanted to get to know whatever she could about him, because she didn't—of course she didn't—but because listening with half an ear did give her time to pull herself together.

The way she looked—braided hair, big round glasses, what shape she did have obliterated by her severely styled suit—didn't matter a jot. It simply wasn't important. The job in hand was the only thing that mattered.

That settled in her mind, she said firmly, 'I had hoped to get straight down to work. But first I need to consult with your fiancée, and she won't be back until this evening, so I'm told.'

She couldn't expect any useful help from him; he had waived all interest, seemingly, giving her an entirely free hand. And his future wife obviously hadn't thought their consultation appointment important enough to keep. Which meant that neither of them could be bothered with details.

Well, that was fine by her—although unusual in her experience. At least it reinforced his promise that she would get no interference, no last-minute changes of mind, throwing everything into turmoil.

But there were things she needed to know before she made progress.

She drained her cup, sighed deeply, and marched back across the room, putting it down on the tray. She hadn't realised that you could actually hear a smile until he said, 'There's no rush. Look on Jan's absence as a bonus and use the time to settle in and relax.'

Relax? How could she when there were a thousand and one things to be done? Had the wretched man, and his equally wretched Janet, no sense of urgency whatsoever? His attitude made her want to scream!

But her biting irritation hadn't penetrated his thick hide; he looked as relaxed as a man could get as he moved to where she was standing. But maybe it had, at that, because he put his cup on the tray and smiled deep into her eyes.

'What do you run on, Alice? Rocket fuel? Slow down. Hyper-efficiency's bad for the health—didn't you know that?'

The backs of his fingers trailed lightly down the side of her face, and this time it wasn't irritation that hit her but a flood of sensation that left her speechless, breathless, rooted helplessly to the spot as he turned his attention back to the coffee-tray.

He refilled her cup and told her, as easily as if nothing had happened, as if the earth hadn't rocked beneath her feet, 'I'll ask Dona to show you the way down at lunchtime.' He moved to the door, his smile very gentle. Or was it pitying? 'That gives you a good hour to unpack and unwind,' he added. 'See you at lunch, Alice.'

She watched him go, her heart still pattering wildly as, unthinkingly, she traced the track of his fingers with hers, then realised what she was doing and despised herself. Thoroughly.

She didn't know what had come over her. Level-headed Alice Rampton going all moony because a man had touched her? Unthinkable!

So he was wickedly attractive and had enough charm to float a battleship. Right. She couldn't dispute that. But she had no business reacting to him in the way she had. He belonged to someone else.

She bit her lip, not liking the way her mind was working. Of course he belonged to someone else! But that really didn't come into it, or shouldn't. And, talking about shouldn't, he shouldn't have touched her in the first place. It wasn't the sort of thing her clients did.

It was all his fault, she rationalised. Her reaction hadn't been—well, what she'd thought it was—but a mix of outrage and downright surprise.

And he shouldn't have taken it on himself to use her first name either. She would have to put a stop to that, politely but firmly.

Staying at her clients' homes for a day or so, where possible and acceptable for them, was expedient all round. It meant that everything could be arranged in double-quick time and obviated the necessity for endless appointments and telephone calls and toing and froing.

But not being a proper guest could cause difficulties, which was why she insisted on formality. She had found it really was the best way.

And in this case it was more important than ever to stick to that rule.

But it shouldn't be. She pulled herself up short, shaking her head at her folly. It was just as important, not more. Making it more made Gideon Rymer different from her other clients, more important. And he wasn't.

To prove it, she thrust him right out of her head and did her unpacking, which took less than five minutes, and after removing her suit jacket and hanging it up she went through to the adjoining bathroom. She acknowledged how splendid it was without allowing a smidgen of envy for the future Mrs Gideon Rymer to surface, washed her hands and made sure her white shirt was neatly tucked into the waistband of her slim grey skirt, then sat on one of the broad window seats in her room, her notepad and pen in her hands, waiting with severely enforced patience for Donatella.

She arrived at exactly two minutes to one. She poked her glossy head round the door.

'Gideon asked me to show you the way down. Ready?' She smiled happily around her. 'Are you comfy here? It's a lovely room, isn't it? But then the whole house is lovely since Gideon took over. You should have seen it before, when he first decided to live here permanently—all dark, dull wallpaper and ugly Victorian furniture. His father wouldn't have a thing changed ever, apparently. Me and Tossie were in on the transformation from the beginning—and Rose, of course. Rose couldn't believe the difference!

And we all worked our socks off. But then who wouldn't, for a man like Gideon?'

And who was Rose? Alice wondered, but couldn't bring herself to ask as she followed the housekeeper along corridors and down the stairs. She was probably another of his groupies. Another raving beauty? Just thinking about it made her head spin. Both the housekeeper and the gardener were in their very early twenties, which made Alice, at twenty-six, feel positively maternal. Had Gideon Rymer put them under some kind of spell?

As she remembered the magic of his eyes, his beguiling smile, his awesome masculine presence and the extremely odd effect he'd had on her practical, down-to-earth self, the idea didn't seem too fanciful.

Donatella opened a panelled wood door onto a light and airy room.

'Through the sitting room and out through the French windows. We're having lunch on the terrace; it's such a lovely day. Everything's ready—I've just got to bring the salads from the kitchen.'

But as Donatella tripped away Alice stood firmly where she was, deeply reluctant to join Gideon for lunch. She would have to, she knew that, but at the moment, for some stupid reason, her heart was fluttering at the mere thought of lunching alfresco, *à deux*.

She needed a few moments to ram some sense into her head. Quiet moments—by herself. She made a dive for the next door along and pushed her way into a huge formal dining room.

Clutching her notepad to her heaving breasts, she leant against the door, her eyes closed. She was behaving like a deranged woman, she knew that, but didn't dwell on it, mentally reinforcing the way she normally saw herself instead. Calm, efficient and determined. Gutsy enough to strike out on her own, start a business from scratch and make a success of it.

And by the time she heard the patter of Donatella's high heels as she returned from the kitchen she had herself under control. She could face Gideon Rymer, no problem.

Her fingers tightened on her notepad as if they were gripping a weapon. She was a professional, wasn't she? So she would use this lunchtime as an opportunity to note down any ideas he had for his wedding. Or any ideas he knew the absent Janet to have. They must have discussed it, for heaven's sake!

Sane again, she waited a few seconds, so that the housekeeper wouldn't see her emerge, then pulled open the door and poked her head round it, checking the coast was clear.

'So there you are,' Gideon said kindly. 'We'd already decided you must have got yourself lost.'

Her heart jumped up into her mouth and she made frantic swallowing movements in her throat, feeling her face go hot and red. He would think she was an idiot and she would have to live with that, because she couldn't tell him what she'd really been doing— psyching herself up to the point when she could face being alone with him.

Gently, but with unmistakable determination, he took her arm, long fingers scalding her skin through the crisp white cotton of her shirt as he led her back towards the door she should have gone through.

'It's this way. Did you tramp through the entire

house, looking for where you should be? Did you feel like Alice in Wonderland, opening doors and finding surprises?'

She wasn't a bit like that Alice! She would have had more sense than to go down the rabbit hole in the first place! And he was laughing at her. She could hear the curl of amusement in his voice and hated it! But there was nothing to be said in her own defence, and, in any case, she doubted if she could have managed more than a squeak.

So she endured his touch, and the rash of goosebumps it brought out all over her body. She was barely aware of the gracious room he was leading her through, her eyes fixed firmly on the light gauze drapes fluttering at the tall French windows, moving gently in the early summer breeze.

His hand left her arm, only to settle, like a brand, on the small of her back as he urged her through onto the terrace.

There was an unmistakable thread of devilment in his rough velvet voice as he invited, 'Come and join the harem, Alice.'

CHAPTER TWO

TOSSIE and Dona sat at a white-covered table, very relaxed, soaking up the sun. Two sexy beauties with Gideon-adoring eyes.

'Hiya!' Tossie beamed. 'Better get stuck in while there's still something left!'

His harem, indeed! There was many a true word spoken in jest—wasn't that what people said?

Alice wondered wildly what the absent Janet thought of it all. His fiancée must be a sublimely beautiful woman, supremely confident in her ability to eclipse these two beauties, otherwise she would have put her foot down and demanded he fire the pair of them, finding replacements over forty, grizzled and preferably male.

The pressure on the small of her back increased, urging her forward, and to escape the unbearable physical contact she shot across the paving slabs and sat down at the table with a bump.

'Help yourself to whatever you fancy,' said Donatella. 'The mushroom risotto is very good.'

Gideon loomed over her and gently unclenched her fingers, removing her notepad from her frenzied grasp, tossing it idly onto a padded lounger.

'You don't need that right now,' he told her smoothly, and she was so aware of the contact, of the brush of his fingers against hers, that she thought she might disintegrate.

If she hadn't been actually experiencing it, she would never have believed it possible.

As far as the male sex went she was unaffecting and unaffected. That was what she had, without rancour, always believed. Yet some cruel, malicious fate seemed intent on proving her wrong.

Unaffecting she certainly still was. But unaffected? Unhappily not. So shattered she scarcely knew what she was doing, she stared blankly at Tossie as she addressed her.

'Settled in?' she asked. 'Did you like your flowers? I did them specially first thing this morning.'

All she could do was summon up a grateful smile, feeling it become fixed and wooden as Gideon took the vacant chair beside her, selected a dish from the many on the table and held it out to her.

Her hand shaking, she helped herself to a little of the risotto. Lecturing herself had done her no good at all. The wretched man had a terrible effect on her, turning her into a person she didn't know.

Thankfully, before that unwelcome admission could make her act even more out of character, he turned his attention to something Tossie was saying, and rather than look at him she looked everywhere else.

There was a serene, archetypically English view over the balustrading—a vista of sweeping, immaculate emerald-green lawns, foaming herbaceous borders and the occasional shade-giving cedar. And nearer at hand the spacious terrace was decked with more profusely planted containers to seduce the senses.

Definitely against her will, her eyes drifted to that

other seducer of the senses. He was enjoying his
lunch, enjoying the light-hearted chatter of the two
beautiful girls, and Alice was relieved to know they
had claimed his attention—because she didn't want
it. It unnerved her too much. But she got it anyway,
the full shattering force of it, as he turned in his seat,
angling his impressive shoulders in her direction.

'Will Gaunt's the only other permanent member of
staff you've yet to meet. I hired him as my land agent
when I took on the running of the Manor estate along
with my own. With my work in chambers and the
courts I couldn't devote the time to make sure that
both estates were managed as they should be. He used
to join the girls for lunch—all one big happy family,
the way it should be—but now more often than not
he takes his lunch break on the job or at home, in
what used to be the gamekeeper's cottage on the
Manor estate.'

She didn't know why he was telling her all this,
and said so, careful to keep her voice light.

'You really don't need to explain anything to me.'
She would have gone on to remind him that a discussion about his wedding-day arrangements would
be far more pertinent, when the way he suddenly
smiled, deep into her eyes, took all her breath away
so she couldn't speak at all.

'Why not? You're going to be part of the big happy
family, as it were, for a couple of weeks, so we ought
to get to know things about each other, don't you
think? I very much look forward to your telling me
something about yourself, Alice, to getting to know
you better.'

A prospect which made her stupid head spin.

'More like two days than two weeks,' she stated firmly, catching her breath back. She lifted her fork then put it back on her barely touched plate again. 'And, while I think about it, I'd prefer it if we kept things formal. I am here on business, after all. Miss Rampton will suit me fine.'

He gave her an awesome white grin, his tanned skin crinkling at the corners of his eyes, heightening the impact of that incredible blue. 'You don't mix business with pleasure, is that it? How very misguided of you, Alice. But while you're here, under my roof, you might learn that it's possible. You might even learn to enjoy it...'

Alice bent her head, trying to hide a sudden rush of colour. Judging by the gorgeous twosome he had working for him, she had little doubt that mixing business with pleasure was high on his agenda.

He was almost flirting with her—plain little Alice Rampton—his lithe, spectacular body angled towards her, his long legs stretched out so that she had to twist hers out of the way to avoid contact.

And she was fully aware of the doting looks Tossie and Donatella skimmed in his direction, even though they were now deep in animated conversation over individual cut-crystal bowls of zabaglione. What the absent Janet thought about his ability to charm any female who came near him she couldn't begin to imagine.

'Alice.' He spoke her name slowly, like a caress. 'It's pretty and soft and feminine. Use it.' He then turned his attention back to where it was appreciated, to his groupies, leaving Alice to dig irately into her risotto. He would do exactly what he wanted, no matter what she said.

She supposed it didn't really matter if he insisted on using her first name. She couldn't afford to get on her high horse and insist he didn't. She couldn't afford to offend him to the point of having him throw her off the job.

Thankfully, the meal appeared to be at an end, and before he could lope away she remarked firmly, 'I have a great deal of work to get through in the next few days, so I wonder, Mr Rymer, if you could show me where you think the marquee should be erected? For your wedding reception, remember?'

She mentally patted herself on the back. She had sounded so crisp and controlled, not the tiniest hint of hesitation or the dreaded fluster that seemed to affect her when he was around. And she drove her point home in the same firm vein.

'When I see the area involved, and get to know how many guests are expected, then and only then can I get on the phone and try to arrange delivery and erection.'

She met his amused blue eyes with a steely gaze, willing herself not to react to the taunt of one upward-drifting dark brow. 'I don't want to be a bore about it, but I promise you, we can't waste time. As it is, we might have left it too late to hire exactly what we want, and I'm sure you'd hate your fiancée to be disappointed.'

'It's Gideon, Alice. That's not too difficult to remember, is it?'

Something twisted sharply inside her. He was doing it again! Forcing an intimacy she didn't want, couldn't begin to cope with!

Glaring at him, she compressed her lips and expelled a sharp breath through her nostrils. She might just as well give up on the matter of what they called each other. She was sensible enough to know when she was well and truly beaten. But if he told her to go back to her room, have a nice little relax and wait until Janet decided she had the time to give her some input she would explode!

She knew, with a great surge of happiness, that she hadn't lost all the battle when he told her, 'I'll be delighted to do what I can, in Jan's absence, to put your mind at rest regarding the location of the marquee.' He leaned back in his chair, one arm casually hooked over the back. 'I am entirely at your disposal.'

His smile was wicked, his eyes even more so, his lithe, supple body provoking sudden and wicked thoughts of her own. Untenable thoughts. Inexcusable thoughts.

She flattened them severely and put on her metaphorical business hat.

That fleeting, quite preposterous moment of wondering what it would be like to snuggle up against that long, indolent body, to rest her head against that wide chest, run her hands along the tanned skin of those very masculine, hard-muscled arms had been if not very laudable then absolutely natural, and nothing to be really, desperately ashamed about.

He was a superlatively attractive male animal, and even though she was boringly plain she possessed all the normal female hormones. It didn't mean she had to give them full rein. Any sort of rein at all.

She got smartly to her feet.

'I'd appreciate that. Thank you for a delicious meal, Dona.' Had anyone noticed she'd barely swallowed a mouthful? She did hope not. She liked the friendly, curvy housekeeper, and didn't want her to think she was unappreciative, rude.

Aware that Gideon was on his feet, she quickly retrieved her notepad. And, with him alarmingly close to her side, she made her way down the flight of steps that led from the terrace, which was full of the sound of the girls' cheerful chatter as they began gathering up the remains of the meal.

At the bottom of the flight of shallow stone steps her feet sank into the soft, closely mown grass that formed an intricate pattern of paths between box-edged, formal rose-beds, the scent and the colour of the massed shrub roses almost overpowering.

Stopping herself from making gushing noises of appreciation, she strode purposefully on, all her muscles tightening as he casually placed a lean, inescapable hand beneath her elbow.

She ached to snatch her arm away, but didn't, because he would put that type of reaction down to the hysterical vapours of the born spinster, who automatically translated any man's most casual, thoughtless touch into an expression of dark and lustful intent, when in reality it was nothing more than disinterested politeness.

So she endured rather than make herself an object of his derision, trying hard to be sophisticated and blasé about it, secure in the knowledge that he had to be completely unaware of the desperate way her heart was jumping around in her chest, making breathing difficult and speech impossible.

'In my father's latter years, the rose garden became an unpruned jungle,' he informed her conversationally. 'But Tossie's done wonders. She grubbed up the lank old lavender hedges and planted box which will take years to make respectable hedging but, she assures me, will be worth the wait. And here—' they had come, at last, to the end of the long central path '—is one of the two lawns I had vaguely in mind.'

'Vaguely' being the operative word, Alice thought resignedly. On the pretext of turning to look back at the house above them, above the billowing sea of roses, she removed her arm from his light-handed grasp and got herself, with difficulty, back into business mode.

The emerald-green lawn—at least an acre of it, she judged—punctuated by the cedars she had noted from the terrace would have been perfect. But...

'Ideally, we should have the marquee closer to the house, in case you're unfortunate enough to have rain on the day. Here, access to the house would have to be through the rose garden, up the steps to the terrace, through the sitting room—'

'Point taken,' he agreed easily, grinning down at her, his thumbs hooked into the pockets of his narrow-fitting jeans, his long legs straddled. 'I admit I haven't given it a great deal of thought. But it appears that a marquee would save total disruption of the household. Gwen, Jan's mother, says it's the traditional thing for a summer wedding, and I have to agree that it would be much better than holding the reception in some anonymous hotel function room, or having guests tramping all over the house. But if this area's out of the question—'

'I didn't say that.'

'You implied it.' He pushed long fingers through his already softly rumpled dark hair and his smile was disarming. 'Well, cast your expert eye over the only other lawn large enough to fit the bill—we go this way.'

He took her hand and loped away, forcing her to trot as they crossed the lawn and dived into a band of dense, tall shrubbery.

He was quite impossible, she thought dizzily, and wondered why Janet Cresswell imagined that he was safe to be left on his own, on the loose. She clutched her notepad to her breast with her free hand and concentrated on keeping her footing. But most of all she put her mind to disregarding the warm pressure of his lean fingers, until she stumbled to a shrieking halt as she tripped over a root and caught her hair in an over-hanging branch.

'Keep still.' He turned immediately, sizing up the situation, a frown of contrition drawing his dark brows together. He steadied her then, his hands firmly on her slender shoulders, and when she tried to pull away, to free herself, he said quickly, 'Don't wriggle, Alice. You'll make it worse.'

For the life of her she couldn't see how it could possibly be worse! He was so close, touching her now, his maleness so daunting, the air beneath the tightly spaced bushes so dark and heated—like the dark heat that surged through her veins.

The silence was intense. Just his slow, steady breathing and the panicky jaggedness of hers.

An involuntary jerk of her head tugged viciously at her trapped hair, making her eyes suddenly swim with tears, and he sucked in his breath.

'It's all right, Alice, don't cry,' he said, his voice soft. 'We'll have you out of this in no time at all.' His long, nimble fingers were working gently to free the bright golden strands of her snagged hair.

'I'm not crying!' she growled. 'I'm not that much of a wimp! Your eyes would water too, if your hair was caught up in a tree!'

'That's my girl!' He grinned down at her. 'Argumentative through thick and thin.' He released the last reluctant strand from its twiggy trap and, to her utter relief, stepped back a pace, allowing her to get her ragged breathing back under some sort of control.

Then he utterly ruined all her tenuously held composure by giving her a long, considering look before remarking, 'Your hair is a uniquely glorious colour. You really shouldn't keep it in that schoolgirl plait.' He tweaked her glasses from her nose and gently wiped the wetness from her cheeks with his fingers. 'I confess I hadn't noticed before, but you have truly beautiful eyes too.'

'Do you talk nonsense to every female you meet?' she snapped at him, hiding behind anger because somehow it was the only reaction she could afford to have.

'You don't like compliments, Alice? Not even if they're sincere?' He tipped his head on one side, the comprehensive slide of his eyes over her slight body minutely assessing.

She ignored what he'd asked and snatched her glasses from his hand. She settled them firmly back in place and suggested stiltedly, 'Let's get on with it, shall we? But take it more slowly this time.'

'I apologise unreservedly for the mishap,' he said, the formality of his words at variance with the devilish glint in his eyes. He gave her a complicated, considering look. 'You go ahead, at your own pace.' He stepped behind her. 'There's a track; just follow that. I run this way regularly each morning. It's the quickest way to the side of the house and the track through the woods leads to the home farm's top pasture.'

So he ran to keep fit. That figured, given his impressively lithe physique. She fixed her eyes on the trodden path that snaked between the bushes. She was glad to have him behind her now. It meant she didn't have to look at him. Looking at him made her feel decidedly uncomfortable with herself, for reasons she had no intention of examining too closely because she didn't dare.

But it meant that he would be looking at her, and that made her wretchedly uncomfortable too. He was surrounded by beautiful women—Tossie and Dona and, it went without saying, Janet Cresswell, the woman he was soon to marry. And she was so darned ordinary. She could just imagine the slightly pitying way he would be looking at her, making the comparison. She was used to that look; she knew it well. She'd seen it countless times when she'd been growing up around those sisters of hers.

She was disgusted with herself, with the way her thoughts kept letting her down. Her spine went rigid, her movements more awkward with every step she took. What was the matter with her, for heaven's sake?

She had spent her growing-up years knowing she couldn't hold a candle to her glamorous sisters and hadn't let it bother her. She hadn't been able to trade on her looks—wouldn't have wanted to either. She had used her intelligence, her ambition, and had made a highly satisfactory life for herself.

So, however unfavourably the man behind her compared her with the others, it was immaterial.

Of course it was.

She heaved a muted sigh of relief when the well-trodden path through the seemingly endless belt of shrubbery opened onto a sweeping lawn, fenced off from a field with cows in it, and beyond and ahead of them she caught a glimpse of the gravel sweep in front of the house, where she had first arrived a few hours ago.

She was back in control now, and thankful for it.

They were close to one of the side elevations of the house and she dipped her head in the direction of an impressive door.

'What's through there? Where does it lead?'

'Nowhere special.' He pushed his hands into the pockets of his thigh-hugging jeans, narrowing his eyes against the glare of the afternoon sun as it bounced back off the white-stuccoed walls. 'Just the garden room and a bath and shower room which used to be a gun room in my grandfather's time. Having no interest in shooting things, I had it converted. It's handy for making myself respectable after my morning's run. The passage leads on into the main hall. Why the interest?'

She had to ignore that question for the moment. A sudden mental image of him stripping off a sweat-stained singlet, jogging pants, and standing under the shower, over six feet of tanned, muscular power, shocked her into pink-cheeked silence.

Blinking fiercely to get rid of the unwelcome, erotic images, she croaked, 'Would you object if it were used as a washroom for your wedding guests? And can you move the cows?'

'No to the first, and yes to the second.' His vivid blue eyes glinted at her. 'Have you any particular objection to cows? Would the poor creatures spoil the illusion of a smart society wedding?'

He was laughing at her, but kindly, as if inviting her to unbend, to share the amusement with him. The warmth of his eyes made her shiver.

Alice averted her own eyes quickly, fixing them on the animals in question. She was beginning to understand and deplore a part of her nature she hadn't known existed until now. She could just about handle the unwanted physical response to this wickedly attractive man, but if she allowed herself to unbend, to enjoy his company, to actually get to like him, she would be in real danger.

She wouldn't allow that to happen.

'Of course not.' She answered his question tartly. She wished he would stop looking at her, smiling at her. She wished he were a million miles away, wished she'd never taken on this commission in the first place.

Her relief at having claimed his time and attention this afternoon had been misplaced. With hindsight she knew it would have been far better if she'd sat around, twiddling her thumbs, waiting for the elusive bride-to-be to put in an appearance.

She had made a start on what she had come here to do, but at the cost of stupidly, self-destructively becoming a victim of his charm, his stunning physical appearance, the shattering charisma of the man.

'Something wrong?' He tipped his dark head, watching the play of fraught emotions as they flooded her pale features. 'Tell me. If you don't think a marquee's the solution then we'll come up with something else. But don't worry about it; it's not important. And don't take everything so seriously.' He lifted a hand as if to touch her, but obviously thought better of it because it dropped slowly back to his side.

Alice shuddered convulsively. If he had touched her she would have ignited.

She shook her head, trying to find words, hoping they'd emerge lucidly, crisply.

'Nothing—nothing's wrong.' She cleared her throat and started again, and this time got it exactly right. 'This is the ideal spot. Close to the house with a convenient washroom for the guests' use, adjacent to the main drive. Without the cows, that field would make a perfect temporary car park.'

She knew she sounded brisk and businesslike, nicely in control, achieving what she'd feared might be impossible. She also knew she'd lost his interest.

Both hands back in his pockets now, his head was averted, his brows drawn down in the very slightest of frowns. He was listening intently, but not to her.

And then she heard it too. The sound of an engine approaching down the long drive, breaking into the tranquil rural silence.

Her salvation, surely? A caller would mean his attention would be diverted. She would be free to go. Free to scurry back to the privacy of her room and give herself a very necessary, stern talking-to.

But knowing what was good for you and wanting it were not at all the same thing, she discovered as her heart plummeted miserably at the prospect.

As the little red car came into sight she lost her reprieve, whether she'd wanted it or not, because he said, with no particular pleasure that she could detect, 'Janet and her mother. Back early. You'd better come and meet them.'

And he didn't sound at all like a man who was eager to join the woman who was supposed to be the love of his life.

CHAPTER THREE

ALICE was introduced to Janet's mother first. Gwen Cresswell was a tiny woman, well into her fifties, with soft wispy grey hair and an anxious line between her eyes.

Janet still had her head in the boot of her car when her mother extended her hand and said, 'You've arrived. That's a relief.'

Alice took the bird-boned hand and wondered if Gwen Cresswell thought Hearts and Flowers was the type of outfit which would blithely accept commissions and then fail to carry them through. She couldn't think of anything else that would explain the other woman's protestations of relief.

'Did you get everything sorted out at the Manor, with the decorators?' Gideon asked his future mother-in-law, seeming only mildly interested.

She shook her head, the frown line deepening. 'I'm afraid not. Everything—well, I couldn't seem to think straight.' She passed her hand over her forehead. 'I'm sorry, but would you both excuse me? I'm getting a headache.'

'Of course, Gwen.' Gideon's eyes mirrored his immediate concern. 'Go and lie down,' he advised. 'Take a couple of painkillers and I'll get Dona to bring you some tea.'

Gwen gave him a grateful smile and walked slowly

into the house, and Gideon turned his attention to his fiancée.

'Weren't you able to help with the decorators, Jan? What was the problem?'

'I didn't go.' Janet Cresswell emerged, clutching a couple of glossy carriers, and closed the boot of the car. 'I dropped Mummy off at home and went on into town.' She looked flustered and evasive, not quite meeting Gideon's eyes, but smiling shyly at Alice. 'You must be Hearts and Flowers. I'm sorry I wasn't here when you arrived. I expect there are a few things you need to know.'

'A few!' Alice smiled warmly, more relaxed now that she could make a proper start on her work. But Janet Cresswell had come as a complete surprise.

Quite a lot younger than Gideon—in her early twenties, Alice decided—she had none of the glamour, polish or stunning good looks she would have expected to find in Gideon's future bride.

Janet was small, slender to the point of thinness, and undeniably plain, with short mousy brown hair tucked behind her ears. Her jeans and checked shirt made no concession to femininity and her lightly tanned face was devoid of make-up. But, Alice noted, she had a lovely smile: rather shy but very sincere, as if she was anxious that people should like her.

One thing was certain: Gideon wasn't marrying her for her looks.

'Perhaps you and Alice could get together this afternoon?' Gideon had moved to his fiancée's side, draping an affectionate arm around her shoulders. 'Alice is the type who feels she has to be hard at work before she can justify the air she breathes.'

'We do need to get things off the ground,' Alice concurred, ignoring his unflattering character assessment, wondering, though, why Janet was so edgy. No one could have missed the way she'd tensed when the man she was shortly to marry had touched her.

'I'm sorry.' Janet moved stiffly from his side, her eyes veiled. 'I'll have to see the decorator, won't I? I thought Mummy would be able to cope.' She shrugged, trying to speak lightly and failing.

'The poor man can't make a start until someone tells him what to do. Mummy wants everything as it was before Daddy died, before the builders replastered. But you know her.' A pale, placating smile was directed at Gideon. 'She's never been able to make a decision in her life, and it's got worse since Daddy died.'

She was already edging round her car. 'I'll see you all at dinner.' She opened the driver's door, saying to Gideon, 'I'm sure you can help Miss—Alice, isn't it?—until I get back.' She slid inside and started the engine.

Gideon, with the first note of impatience in his voice, turned to Alice and asked, 'What do you need to know that's so vital?'

Give me patience! Alice fumed inwardly, dragging a deep breath in through her nostrils before informing him tartly, 'I have to know how many guests you are inviting.' Then she softened her tone, because in her experience most men didn't have a clue about the work that went into organising a wedding, and he wouldn't be any different.

'It affects everything—the size of the marquee, the number of invitations I have to get printed, the numbers to be catered for.' She saw his dark brows bunch together and assured him, a smile in her voice now, at his very male perplexity, 'Just the guest list. After that, I won't need to trouble you again.'

'Right.' He pivoted lightly on his feet. 'Let's get it over with.' And he set off towards the house with a loose-limbed stride that had Alice trotting to keep up.

They went in through the main door and across the spacious hall. He paused at one of the doors then pushed it open. 'Wait in here. I'll be two seconds.'

Alice was in the sitting room again, catching her breath. For a man who was so laid-back and relaxed, he could certainly behave like a whirlwind when he wanted to.

Alone, she felt a little easier, a little more in control. It was his presence that fazed her, she knew. Just looking at him made her feel things she didn't want to have to face. She wished she could find something about him she could actively dislike—despise, even.

Sighing, she allowed the elegant proportions of the room to relax her. It was flooded with golden sunlight, the festoons of hazy fabric still fluttering at the open French windows, the soft air scented by the many bowls of stately white lilies.

And then Gideon was back, changing everything. The air was spiky now, seeming to abrade her skin, making her breath catch sharply in her throat.

It was something she had no control over, and she hated it. She hated it even more when he gave her that wicked smile of his, said, 'Catch!' and dropped down at one end of a pale lemon silk-upholstered sofa and patted the empty cushion at his side.

She didn't want to sit anywhere near him; her control was precarious enough as it was. But to take herself off to the far end of the room and peer at him from a distance would be to make herself utterly ridiculous.

Clutching the squat leather-bound book he had lobbed in her direction, she approached the sofa and perched on the edge of the squashy cushion, watched by his lazily amused eyes.

'My address book,' he told her. 'Hang onto it as long as you need. But I thought I should stay around while you flip through it, in case you can't decipher my handwriting.'

His handwriting. His book. Touching one of his belongings was like touching him. Intimate. Somehow shocking. The feel of the soft leather binding beneath her fingers made her dizzy.

He moved slightly, stretching out his long legs, and the fabric pulled tight against the hard muscles of his thighs. He casually rested an arm along the top of the sofa behind her and she felt swamped, overwhelmed by the nearness of him, by the essence of the man himself, an essence so strong it seemed to penetrate every last pore of her skin.

Mortified by her reactions, she made herself open the book. She was the one who had insisted they couldn't afford to waste any more time, she reminded herself.

She stabbed her glasses further up her nose and concentrated. Slashing black pen strokes, firm and decisive—decipherable, with care.

A healthy scattering of QCs, a couple of eminent judges, a few single male names and some couples—

associates, friends, distant cousins, whatever—and rather more than a few single females.

She would have to ask him, distasteful though it might be. So many female names and addresses. It would be too crass for words if she sent wedding invitations to a whole bunch of former girlfriends. Or lovers. She cleared her throat.

'There appears to be a largish number of unattached females.' How stiff she sounded, how disapproving, even to her own ears! She ploughed on. 'Do you want me to have invitations sent to them?'

He put back his head and roared with laughter, making hot colour fly to her face, then sobered just as abruptly, his eyes narrowed on her flushed features.

'You're an odd little thing, Alice. Wise up, why don't you? Do you really think I'd invite a flock of lady friends to my own wedding?' The deep blue of his eyes was suddenly teasing, his voice a suave drawl. 'Wouldn't I keep such private names and telephone numbers in another little black book entirely?'

There was no answer she could give to that. She felt her face burn with mortification. He probably enjoyed making her feel foolish, painfully unsophisticated. And, she noted, he hadn't said *ex*-lady friends!

So did the private little black book exist? He had as good as implied that it did, and she suspected it did. So was that, then, the first brick she could use in the wall of dislike she self-protectively needed to erect?

She was saved from further speculation or comment by the arrival of Dona with a tea-tray. She put it on the low table in front of them then planted her small hands on her curvy hips and smiled engagingly at Gideon.

'I took tea to Mrs Cresswell, as you asked. But she didn't want it. I don't suppose she'll make it down for dinner; she's probably getting one of her migraines. Shall I lay it in the morning room for eight o'clock as usual, or out on the terrace?'

Had she any idea how tantalisingly she smiled, how provocative her stance was? Alice wondered as Gideon watched his housekeeper with hooded eyes, his mouth curving softly.

She couldn't read Dona's mind, couldn't decide whether the girl was being deliberately provocative or was simply just gorgeous and innocently unaware of her effect. But she could read her own, and she knew that only a few short hours ago she would have tartly reminded herself that it was none of her business, whereas now—now she felt annoyed on Janet Cresswell's behalf.

The sisterhood of the plain woman, she supposed, inwardly wincing at the dreariness of the thought.

'We'll have dinner on the terrace, please, while this weather holds.' His smile shimmered into wickedness. 'You know how I enjoy doing the things I like in the great outdoors.'

Dona giggled infectiously at that as she left the room, her hips swinging coquettishly, and Alice watched her disapprovingly. She really liked Dona, and that went for Tossie too, and she would dearly like to believe that their free and easy behaviour with their employer stemmed merely from the fact that they were friendly and open and very young—like a pair of affectionate puppies.

But with a man like Gideon you could never be sure. Look at the way she herself had—

She refused to follow that train of thought, and busied herself with the tea things. She'd drink a cup then make her escape.

Passing him his cup, she found him watching her intently, as if he was trying to see behind her prim façade, wondering what made her the woman she was. The look unnerved her, and her hand shook as she picked up her own cup so she put it straight down again.

It was a gift he had—if you could call it that. He'd obviously been born with the ability to blow the brains of the female of the species into orbit. The unfairness of it was that plain women were no more immune than beautiful ones.

That Gideon Rymer appreciated beauty in all its forms was shown in the things he surrounded himself with. In a very short space of time he had turned what had apparently been a dreary, over-furnished home into a place of loveliness and light, neglected gardens into a fantasy of flowers. Rymer Court wasn't the home of a man who didn't care about his surroundings.

And the women who worked for him were beautiful too.

Yet he was marrying a plain girl.

Alice quickly gathered up her notepad and pen, and the address book he'd loaned her. She couldn't bear his silent scrutiny a moment longer, nor the way her thoughts kept homing in on him.

'You have everything you need?'

Against her will her eyes were tugged in his direction. He was still lounging there, as relaxed as only a man who had everything going for him, and knew it, could be.

She didn't have everything she needed. She needed her equilibrium back, her sense of purpose, her precious detachment. He had stolen all that from her, and more, but she couldn't ask him to give it back.

'Everything except the guest list from your fiancée's side,' she said stiltedly. Without that she could still do nothing useful, and suddenly her need to be finished up here and back in her own environment was much more than good business sense, it was the most important thing in her life.

Her tone must have betrayed her agitation, because he lifted his hands with graceful apology. 'I can't help you there. Now if Rose had been here you would be finished up by suppertime and on your way. She's ultra-efficient, my no-nonsense Rose!'

There was a definite note of affection in his voice, and she'd heard that name mentioned before. Although she knew she simply didn't want to know—to hear that Rose was an ultra-efficient secretary, perhaps, and another raving beauty—she asked, 'And who is Rose?'

She took up her teacup again, to drink the cooling liquid, and admitted to having acquired more than a veneer of cynicism when he confounded her with his answer.

'My stepmother. Though the ''step'' bit doesn't come into it. As far as I'm concerned, she had me when I was four years old, when she married my father.'

Her eyes widened behind her owly glasses. It

seemed so sad that he should write his real mother off so offhandedly. Even if he couldn't properly remember her, surely she deserved a special, inviolable place in his heart?

'You must have been very young when your mother died,' she muttered, perhaps a shade tartly, and his brows drew together as if she'd spoken in a foreign language and he was trying to make sense of incomprehensible words.

'Do you always make such wild assumptions?' His voice was harsh. She felt his disapproval like the points of a thousand darts. 'My biological mother didn't die until I was twelve years old, when she was drowned with her third husband in a speed-boat accident off Cannes.

'She walked out on us a couple of months before my second birthday. If the portraits stashed away in the attics are anything to go on, she was a breathtakingly beautiful woman. Living here, she didn't have nearly enough of an audience, enough besotted men to pay the homage she felt was due to her beauty. So she left. That was the general consensus of opinion, or so I'm told.

'Dad divorced her but never stopped loving her. He became very bitter. But he eventually married Rose, his housekeeper, and it was the most sensible thing he ever did. She hasn't a vain or flighty bone in her body. She gave me a stable, happy home life, and—until I was in my early teens and capable of standing up for myself—was a buffer between me and my father. He was a cold, domineering man, with a gift for making inspired investments. In the end it was the only thing he thought of.'

'Where is Rose now?' Was that her voice? Gentle, a soothing verbal caress, flooded with sympathy. He had said his father was an embittered man. Did he realise that some of it had rubbed off on him? Was he emulating the 'most sensible thing' his father had ever done, in choosing a plain, wholesome bride, leaving the beautiful butterflies to flutter where they would at will?

'Having the time of her life, or so I hope.' He got to his feet and Alice noted the way the sleek thigh muscles flexed beneath the soft, hugging fabric of his jeans. She closed her eyes, her breath shaky in her lungs, and heard him speak again, his tone warm, loving.

'Following my father's death, and the alterations I put in hand here, I insisted she took a break. She's visiting a sister and her family out in Canada. She'll be back in time for the wedding, and after that she'll be moving to the Manor to live with Gwen. It will be ready for occupation when the decorators move out.' He was walking towards the door, and her eyes were following him. 'It was her idea. She and Gwen have been friends for years and she insisted that newly weds need time to themselves.'

Alice pretended an enormous interest in the fingers that were clenched so painfully tightly around her notepad. The mere thought of him being newly wedded to anyone caused a deep and anguishing pain.

When she found the courage to raise her eyes again the room was empty.

Ten minutes later she closed her bedroom door behind her, leaned limply back against it and pressed her fingertips to her throbbing temples.

No point in asking what was wrong with her. She knew the answer only too well. She had come here to organise a wedding and in a few short hours had become infatuated with the groom!

Bathed, her hair washed, brushed and freshly braided, Alice made her way downstairs for dinner, at eight, on the terrace.

She was wearing what she privately called one of her wallpaper dresses—a short-sleeved grey shift, guaranteed to make her fade into the background, something she always considered it best to do when dining with clients, *en famille*.

She was perfectly calm now, the wild silliness of her infatuation rationalised. She had forced herself to review everything she knew about the man and had reached the satisfying, self-protecting conclusion that he was to be despised.

He had referred to his wedding as a circus and an illusion. He had cold-bloodedly decided to marry a plain girl because she would be unlikely to be tempted to stray, and meanwhile he kept his own very private little black book of names and phone numbers and surrounded himself with a couple of gorgeous, openly doting female employees to add a little spice to his home life.

And, if that weren't enough to put him at the head of the list for the Louse of the Year Awards, she was pretty damn sure property came high on his list of desirable assets to be sought in a bride.

She had already gleaned that since the death of Janet's father he'd been running the Manor lands along with his own. And as his future bride was an only child then the house and the lands would come to her in the fullness of time. Valuable assets, both.

He was wealthy in his own right, but obviously more than bitterness had rubbed off from his father. He too had the need to acquire more, and more again.

So the juvenile infatuation in itself wasn't a real danger, because she wouldn't be here for long and could make herself cope with it, see it as the folly it was. And as soon as she was away from here, from him, that physical attraction would go the way of all ephemera and obligingly fade away.

But she had been growing to like him. Add that to the attraction and what did you get?

The unthinkable.

But despising him, as she would despise any man who could choose a bride so cold-bloodedly, simply to save himself the hassle of keeping her faithful to him and to get his hands on a chunk of valuable property, negated that danger.

And at least Janet would be joining them for dinner, and afterwards they could go into a huddle and get the guest list finalised.

The table on the terrace was laid buffet-style. Wine in a silver ice bucket, cold pheasant, green salad, a cold golden courgette omelette, peaches poached in red wine, a huge selection of cheeses. Enough food to feed a small army. And no one there to eat it.

She felt like a spare part, and was uncomfortable with that, but the physical sensations that bombarded her when she saw Gideon walking up the steps from the gardens below were more than merely uncomfortable, they were terrifying.

She felt giddy, her heart thumping madly, enough

to choke her. He looked fantastic in thigh-hugging stone-coloured lightweight trousers and a black silk shirt.

Surreptitiously, she wiped her suddenly damp palms down the sides of her dress and wished herself a million miles away. So much for her protestations that she could cope with mere physical attraction.

At eighteen, doing business studies, she'd dated a fellow student, flattered by his interest because, where romance was concerned, she'd lived in the shadow of her sisters and had aroused no interest in anyone. His advances had gone to her head and she'd believed herself madly in love. Almost inevitably she had gone to his bed, and had found the experience nothing spectacular. Interest had quickly waned on both sides and, since then, she'd been too level-headed, too career-minded to allow herself the folly of being knocked sideways by mere physical male attributes.

Until now.

She straightened her spine. She was simply going to have to ignore whatever it was about this man that made her mouth go dry, made her heart leap like a landed fish. And she was almost sure she could manage it until he reached the top of the steps and smiled down at her, his head tipped a little to one side.

'Hungry, Alice?'

'Yes.' Her voice was thick. All her carefully catalogued reasons for despising him had flown straight out of her head. She was hungry, desperately hungry, but not for food.

The magic of his smile had pushed all her sternly sensible resolutions into limbo. She craved to touch him, hold him, kiss that sensual mouth. She yearned to discover what it would be like to be held in those strong arms, held closely against that unbelievably sexy body, to have his lips taste her skin, possess her own. And it was madness... Wickedness... Unthinkable...

'Good. It's help yourself time, by the look of it. Dig into whatever you fancy while I pour the wine.'

Thank God he hadn't noticed anything peculiar about her, Alice thought with a fervour that shook her, made her teeth clench together. At least that proved she had enough self-control to stop her emotions from actually showing, and shaming her.

She followed him over to the table, her wretched legs shaky, and put a slice of the golden omelette on a plate, with a little green salad. She gladly sat down, and with considerable will-power she made her voice light.

'Where is everyone?' When Janet arrived she would break the tension. Gideon seemed unaware of it, thankfully, but it was winding her up to the point of explosion.

'They've deserted us.' He was moving around, heaping his plate. The sun was much lower in the sky now, slanting across the terrace, gilding the dark hairs on the firm, tanned flesh of his arms, touching the starkly beautiful planes of his face with a loving, golden caress.

She looked away quickly, self-disgust staining her cheeks, painfully, achingly aware of him as he dropped easily into the seat beside her and elaborated.

'Gwen's headache developed into a full-blown migraine—no doubt brought on by her inability to instruct the decorators—and Jan phoned to say that a

call came through for her while she was at the Manor
from a schoolfriend she hasn't seen in years. She's
passing through the area on her way to the Midlands
and they wanted to catch up on each other's news.
So Jan's meeting her for a ploughman's at the George
and Dragon in the next village but one. It's only a
mile or so off the motorway. She sends her apologies
and says she'll see you in the morning.'

He smiled at her, that lovely, lazy smile of his.
'You wouldn't have achieved anything of much sig-
nificance this evening anyway. Better to leave everything until you're both fresh in the morning.'

But Alice, for once, wasn't inwardly screaming
with impatience at this further delay, as he obviously
expected her to be. She was thinking that if she'd
been Janet, engaged to marry this man—whatever his
motives—she wouldn't have been flitting hither and
thither all day, taking no interest whatsoever in her
wedding arrangements. She'd have been glued to his
side, never letting him move further than she could
see him.

Which only went to prove what a disastrous effect
Gideon Rymer had on her, she mourned.

She tried to edge her chair a little further away
without him noticing, and tried to eat some of the
food she'd given herself. But her throat had closed up
and she couldn't swallow. She gave up the attempt,
laid down her fork and, desperate to break the suddenly stinging silence, asked, 'The others? Tossie and
Dona?'

She was mentally crossing her fingers, stupidly
hoping that by speaking of them she could magic
them up out of thin air so she wouldn't have the pain-

ful pleasure of being alone with him. But his reply
dashed her hopes.

'The girls don't eat with us in the evening.' He
helped himself to more cold pheasant, oblivious to the
way he affected her—which was a comfort, she con-
soled herself as he went on, 'Lunch is a moveable
feast. Sometimes we all eat together, sometimes not.
It depends who's around. And they do need time
off—their evenings to themselves. Tossie and Dona
share the flat about the stable block.

'So...' He was leaning back in his chair. 'I seem
to have done all the talking in our short relationship.'
He was slightly angled, looking directly into her face,
twisting the stem of his wineglass idly in his long
fingers, the soft warmth in his remarkable eyes inviting confidences, hinting at an intimacy that was unbearable because it was so tempting. 'Your turn now.
Why don't you tell me something about yourself?'

'I don't think so.' A decisive jab of her forefinger
settled her glasses more firmly on her nose. She
jumped to her feet. She couldn't afford the dangerous
indulgence of an intimate tête-à-tête. Smoothing
down her dress, she told him, 'An early night for me,
I think. Down to work in the morning, bright and
early.'

She had sounded like an obnoxious schoolmistress
and was proud of herself. She was proud of the way
she had refused to give in to the temptation to stay,
and of the way she didn't show any reaction now,
when he displayed all the magic of that devastating
smile of his, uncoiling himself like a lazy panther as
he got to his feet, then looking down at her with an

odd, reflective expression in his eyes for a long, silent moment.

'Fair enough,' he said at last. 'Then I'll take the opportunity to tackle some of the work that's piling up in my study.' He made a slight 'after you' gesture, ushering her through to the sitting room. 'If you need the use of a fax machine, there's one in the study. Feel free, any time. Shall I show you where to find it? Or will the morning be soon enough?'

'The morning.' Her voice made it sound as if she was being strangled. Why did he have to affect her so powerfully? She had to escape!

She was breathless when she reached the sanctuary of her room. But restless. She knew she wouldn't sleep.

She hadn't thought to bring a book, seeing no need, having imagined herself sitting up this evening, making detailed and copious notes of people to be contacted in the morning. But since deciding on the site for the marquee was all she had accomplished she had nothing to write notes about!

A brisk walk would go some way to working off her restless frustration, she decided. The long, early summer evening was still lovely, and she replaced her plain court shoes with her sturdy driving shoes and crept very quietly out of the silent house, scarcely daring to breathe in case Gideon heard her and came to investigate.

She didn't want to have to see him again unless it was safely in the company of others, when she could, with some hope of success, try to pretend he wasn't there.

It was so peaceful here, and tranquil. She would

sleep now, and tomorrow was another day. A better day. Not so unsettling, surely?

She actually managed a satisfactory little yawn as she rejoined the drive and walked towards the house. And then the lovely peace was shattered as Janet's car roared up the drive with a stab of headlights and a ragged splatter of gravel.

She fully expected to see her emerge from the parked car and scamper into the house to spend what was left of the evening with her fiancé. But she didn't. She was still sitting there, hunched over the steering wheel, staring straight ahead, when Alice drew level.

She poked her head through the open window. 'Are you OK?' Janet didn't look well. Her face was ashen, her unremarkable features set and stony. Alice thought she'd been crying but couldn't be sure because the light was rapidly fading.

'Oh, hello again. No, I'm fine, really.' Janet removed the key from the ignition and Alice stood back as the other girl got out of the car.

She looked so forlorn and lost that Alice wanted to ask her what was wrong, but she knew she couldn't presume, so said instead, to cheer her up, 'We'll have a great day tomorrow. You can tell me exactly how you see your wedding and leave me to translate your fantasy into fact, and—'

She was left on the drive, her mouth gaping, as the bride-to-be burst into tears of anguish and rushed headlong into the house.

CHAPTER FOUR

BREAKFAST was served in the kitchen.

'To save Dona's legs,' Gideon explained from his seat next to Janet at the big scrubbed pine table, when Alice came down and found where they all were.

'There is nothing wrong with my legs!' Dona hiked her short skirt even higher, giggling, displaying the utter perfection of the limbs in question, and Gideon reached out an arm and wrapped it cosily around her tiny waist, grinning at her.

'Utterly gorgeous, as you know very well! And that's the way we want to keep them.'

Lascivious lout! Alice resisted the impulse to slap him. Ogling the hired help, cuddling her in front of the girl he was next door to marrying! And Donatella ought to have known better, with poor Janet sitting there witnessing the giggly, flirtatious leg-show!

But Janet, between Gideon and Gwen at the breakfast table, didn't appear distressed. She was even smiling a little, and there was a definite look of mischief in her eyes as she advised, 'Don't knock it, Dona. Take all the concern the man offers—you don't want to end up with varicose veins and bunions, do you?'

With a wild little shriek at the thought of such a fate, Dona spun round to the Aga and removed a bubbling pan, then went round the table spooning boiled eggs into flowered china cups while Gwen, apparently completely recovered, launched into a gory tale about a dear friend of hers who had suffered so very terribly with veins.

Alice closed her ears and sliced the top off her egg, wondering about Janet. She had seemed to take the floor show in her stride and she did look better this morning, more composed.

Alice had lain awake long into the night, pondering the possible reason for the bride-to-be's outburst of sobs and tears. A simple case of pre-wedding nerves? A bit early in the day for that, surely?

Or something much worse? Like being deeply in love with Gideon, longing desperately to be his wife, yet suspecting—or knowing—he was playing around and would probably continue to indulge the bad habit after the wedding? Suspecting he was marrying her for selfish, mercenary reasons alone?

She had fallen asleep without reaching a conclusion, because she had no hard proof of anything, but at least the exercise had taken her mind off the way she so totally and helplessly responded to the wretched man. Body, and—if she didn't watch it— heart and mind.

She was seated opposite him at the table, and even though she kept her eyes on her plate she could have given a detailed description of exactly how he looked, what he was wearing. A long-sleeved T-shirt that lovingly moulded his torso was tucked into scuffed blue jeans secured by a narrow leather belt, with a chunky steel buckle that...

Alice gulped, choking on a corner of buttered toast. She didn't know what made her think things like that—didn't know what had come over her, what was happening to her.

Well, to be truthful, she did know. And didn't like it. She wished she'd handed this commission over into her assistant's perfectly capable hands.

Then things got slightly better. Gwen had stopped talking about veins and Tossie breezed in, looking vital and gorgeous in her next-to-nothing shorts, topped this morning by a shirt that would have been respectable if most of the buttons hadn't been left undone.

'There's a bit of a ground mist this morning, but when the sun gets through it's going to be another scorcher.' She perched on the end of the table near Dona, who was settling down to her own breakfast, and poured two mugs of tea from the pot. 'Will's just opening up the estate office. He looks like a bear with the proverbial, so I said I'd take a cuppa across.'

'I'll do it.' Janet was on her feet. 'Stay and drink your tea, Toss.' She took one of the brimming mugs and her face was slightly pink as she hooked her short brown hair back behind her ears with her free hand.

'Don't forget we've got a lot to get through this morning,' said Alice quickly, afraid she might take off for the day again.

'What?' Janet was already at the outer kitchen door, the one that led to the passage to the courtyard and the stable block. She turned, frowning, then smiled the beautiful smile that made her look so very attractive. 'No, of course not. Ten minutes, I promise. In the sitting room.' And she was gone.

Gideon took his narrowed eyes from his future wife and asked, 'Finished, Alice?'

She nodded, her eyes sliding quickly away from him.

'Then I'll take you to my study, so you'll know where it is if you want to use the fax.'

She rose reluctantly. She would have given anything to be able to say, No, thanks, someone else can point me in the right direction. But she couldn't do that. For all he appeared to treat life lightly, he was highly intelligent, a first-rate barrister, and wondering why she avoided his company would be only one short step away from his hitting the truth.

The humiliation if he were to discover her guilty secret would be unendurable.

Away from the comings and goings, the breakfast-time chatter of the kitchen, Gideon's study, dark-panelled and masculine, was an oasis of peace. Or should have been, Alice corrected as her nerves skittered about when he casually took her arm and guided her to a desk tucked away in the chimney alcove where the fax and a telephone lived.

'And there's a typewriter on my desk.' The big mahogany desk was scattered with legal-looking documents tied up with tape. 'Or, if you prefer, you could use the PC in the estate office. Will won't mind; he swears he can't get the hang of the thing and avoids it like the plague. As a land agent he's top drawer, but his office skills are non-existent. I'm going to have to put him out of his misery and hire him a part-time secretary.'

Alice tried to control her breathing. Her eyes were misting up with tears. He was so easy to be with, so open, so confident and relaxed with himself that he had no difficulty at all in discussing details of his life with a comparative and, let's face it, not very forth-coming stranger.

Could he possibly be the monster she was doing her damnedest to make herself believe he was? Could he really be the immoral womaniser of her wild im-aginings, the type of man who would cold-bloodedly marry for mercenary reasons?

Thankfully, he released her arm to consult his watch, and a deep shudder of reaction snaked through her as the much too intimate warmth of his hand was removed.

His gaze suddenly narrowed, probing through the defence of her owly glasses. Then slowly, with intent deliberation, his eyes swept down to rest on her parted lips, then back to look deep into her eyes, a tiny query in the shards of glittering blue. To hide the answer, she turned her head sharply.

She heard him let out a soft breath before he told her, 'I'm going into chambers later today, and I have a circuit dinner tonight. You won't need any more immediate input from me?'

The faint frown had gone from between his eyes. His face was impassive, the face of a stranger, telling her nothing. It was as if that fraught moment of soul-searching had never happened. She almost shouted, No, I don't need you in any way, shape or form! so great was the initial relief of knowing he'd be out of the way for the rest of the day. And with any luck, and a lot of hustling, she would be on her way back to base before the end of tomorrow.

But the relief was short-lived, because the next thing she felt was the draining weight of deep dis-appointment. Of loss.

Fool! she growled savagely at herself, and forced out thinly, 'I need nothing more from you, Mr Rymer.'

Mortified, she watched one dark brow rise sardonically. 'Sure about that, Alice?' he wanted to know, and then ushered her politely out of the room. 'Run along, then.'

Dismissed. And, worse than that, secretly laughed at! And rumbled? Oh, surely to heaven not!

He closed the door on her, leaving her feeling flushed and foolish. And in no mood to organise his wretched wedding!

But that was what she was being paid handsomely to do. And of course she was professional enough to get on with it. She could disregard what she suspected about his morals—only a whisker away from non-existent—and push the unfortunate, shattering physical effect he had on her firmly out of the way.

Janet was waiting, as promised, in the sitting room, curled up on one of the sofas, her legs tucked under her. Alice paused, her notebook at the ready, the design portfolios tucked securely under one arm, suddenly swamped with guilt. The younger girl looked so vulnerable, her smile so trusting. What would she think if she knew her wedding consultant was secretly lusting after her husband-to-be?

It didn't bear thinking about. It made her feel contemptible. To counter it, she pulled herself together and imparted briskly, the complete professional now, 'Mr Rymer gave me a list of the people he would like invited to your wedding. If I could have yours?'

Her smile was cool, impersonal, but it slipped a

little when Janet merely gave an offhand shrug and muttered, 'I suppose.'

Fixing the smile back in place, Alice perched on the sofa opposite and flipped open her notepad, pen poised. She knew what it would feel like to be swimming upstream in a river of treacle but, at the end of a couple of hours or so, the list was finalised at a hundred and fifty.

'I'll get the marquee organised,' Alice confirmed, 'and the invitations printed and sent out. I'll arrange with my usual florist for the decorations and the flowers for the wedding itself; I'll also take care of food, wines, photographers and cars. Now, which would you prefer for the evening—a lively disco or a discreet string quartet? Or a mixture of both? You know the ages and preferences of your guests; I don't.'

'Better ask Gideon.' Janet shrugged, then heaved a great sigh. 'You know, I envy you—a proper business of your own, a real job to do. It must give you a lot of satisfaction.' She twisted the hem of her T-shirt between her fingers, then smoothed out the consequent folds. She seemed nervous, agitated, deliberately turning the conversation away from her wedding.

Alice watched her closely, sucking her lower lip between her teeth. In her experience, brides couldn't stop talking about what they wanted.

'I did a secretarial course, you know,' Janet confided. 'I got quite good and had dreams about becoming some high-flyer's PA. Then everything went wrong. Daddy got sick, and Mummy simply couldn't cope, so I stayed home. Then, when Daddy had that fatal accident, she needed me even more. Then

Gideon's father died shortly after, and then…' Her eyes suddenly pooled with tears but she blinked them impatiently away. 'Well, then we decided to marry, and that was that. So I guess all that training went down the plughole.'

So Janet was a closet career woman. Was that the problem? Did part of her want to marry and yet another part yearn to make her own way in life?

'It needn't be a waste,' said Alice, thinking on her feet, remembering what Gideon had said about the estate manager's office skills. 'Mr Rymer was telling me earlier that he would have to employ a part-time secretary in the estate office. Why don't you apply for the job? People might say it was nepotism, but what the hell? You'd be using your valuable skills and you, your husband and—Will, isn't it?—would know you were doing a great job!'

It seemed like a wonderful idea to her, and if the future Mrs Gideon Rymer were gainfully employed then she might stop looking so darned miserable.

But Janet stared at her as if she'd suggested something outrageous, her face draining of colour as she whispered, 'That wouldn't be possible.'

Why not? Because Gideon was the type of man who would refuse to allow his wife the satisfaction of holding down a job, having a degree of independence? Did he expect any wife of his to be totally dependent, subjugated to his will?

Suddenly she felt sorry for the girl, trapped by her fascination for the heartless devil. She herself was being drawn into that particular web, so she could understand what poor Janet was going through.

But she herself could get away, out of here, could

remove herself from the danger. And would waste no time in doing so.

'It was just a thought,' she dismissed with a smile, and added briskly, 'Just one more thing, and then you can leave all the work to me. The wedding dress. And how many bridesmaids are you having?'

'None. And I'll pick up something in the way of a dress in town some time.'

Pick up something? Alice was appalled.

Even if Gideon was marrying her for dubious reasons, seeing her as little more than a cipher—a loyal, undemanding wife who would give him children, no trouble, and, eventually, an enormously valuable chunk of property—then behaving like a rag doll that had been left out in the rain, showing no spirit at all, was not the way to go about altering the situation.

If she were in poor Janet's shoes she would be fighting her corner, determined to make the very best of herself and her coming marriage. And she'd start off by presenting him with a bride he could be proud of, could actually begin to fall in love with!

Shattered by the smouldering vehemence of her thoughts, the pictures she had conjured up of herself in white satin and lace, smiling dreamily up at Gideon Rymer as he slipped a plain gold band on her own wedding finger, Alice got hold of herself sharply and said darkly, 'That won't do!' Meaning both her own mawkish imaginings and Janet's hopelessness. 'It's going to be your big day and it's going to be very special, and you're going to look fantastic.'

And with Tossie and Dona in the congregation and at the reception—both of whom were guaranteed to look stunning even if dressed in nothing more glamorous than old doormats—poor Janet would need all the help she could get.

'I have a couple of young, highly talented designers on my books,' she explained, trying to arouse some enthusiasm. 'They specialise in fabulous wedding gowns. I have their portfolios right here. Look through them, and if you like what you see pick which designer you think you prefer and I'll arrange for him to get down here for a consultation.'

She rose with smooth efficiency and put the bound sheaves of design drawings and photographs down on the coffee-table. But Janet made no attempt to pick them up, merely commenting indifferently, 'If that's what you want.'

Alice held her breath and counted to ten. It wasn't what she wanted, dammit! Seeing Janet wearing a fabulous wedding gown and walking down the aisle on Gideon's arm wasn't what she wanted at all!

She flattened the treacherous thought. She had to be a professional here, and her own secret, guilty wants and needs didn't come into it. And as Janet's wedding consultant there was something she had to know.

Taking her seat again, she crossed one leg neatly over the other and composed her features into what she hoped was a semblance of sympathetic patience.

'I have to ask you this,' she said firmly. 'Do you want this marriage to go ahead, or am I wasting my time and Mr Rymer's money?'

She watched as Janet's face went a violent red. 'What do you mean? Why do you ask?' She looked hunted and haunted.

'I ask because, so far, you've shown an unusually

low level of interest in the arrangements and no enthusiasm at all,' Alice pointed out levelly. And then, as she watched the other woman's face go deadly pale, she added gently, 'My gut feeling tells me there's something wrong, that for some reason you're not entirely happy.' The tears of anguish last night had said it all, hadn't they? 'Wouldn't it help to talk it through?'

'I—I—' Janet stuttered wretchedly, her fingers knotted together in her lap. 'There's nothing. Really. I've known Gideon always—since as far back as I can remember. He's a wonderful man. I think the world of him, honestly I do! And of course the wedding's going ahead!'

'In that case, why don't you look at the portfolios?'

Alice swallowed around the lump in her throat. The outburst had affected her deeply, strangely, indicating irrefutably that what she felt for Gideon Rymer was not the mere infatuation of a long-time celibate woman for a lust-worthy man, but something far, far worse.

Janet couldn't hide her wretchedness. She was deeply in love with a man who was callously using her, and determined to go through with the marriage at all costs, even though she knew the price she was going to have to pay, all because she wasn't strong enough to cut her love for him out of her heart and walk away.

It made him the monster Alice had tried to convince herself he was. And now she *was* convinced. And it hurt. Hurt unbelievably.

And precisely because of that she knew that deep,

deep down she had wanted to believe in his integrity, hadn't wanted to fall helplessly in love with a louse!

Love? Was this what the pain was about?

Her eyes half-closed in misery, she barely registered the way Janet was dutifully flipping through the pages, scarcely noticed Dona as she carried a tray of coffee things through to the terrace.

Her instinct was to get away. Right away. Now. Crawl back to her own home and lick her wounds and try to get over what she felt for him the best she could. Her austere living quarters suddenly seemed like the best possible place in the world to be.

For a few moments she actually pondered ways and means, and the necessary exercise in damage limitation. She could invent a phone call, a sick relative, and send Rachel, her capable assistant, here in her stead. But in the end she knew she couldn't do that.

She wasn't a quitter, and she'd be damned if she'd let Gideon Rymer turn her into one! There was a job to be done and she would do it.

'I'm sorry.' Janet was hovering over her, had spoken to her and she hadn't heard a word. 'I was miles away.'

'Dona's brought coffee; we're having it outside. Coming?'

The sun had broken through the mist and it was another glorious day. Tossie and Dona were already there, munching chocolate biscuits.

And so was Gideon.

Gideon looking unbearably sexy in business gear. A lightweight grey suit with a faint pinstripe, crisp white shirt and a sober dark blue tie. He was lounging back in one of the cast-iron, white-painted chairs, a leather briefcase and an overnight bag near his immaculately shod feet.

His presence came as a shock. She hadn't seen him pass through the sitting room; she'd been lost in the dark labyrinths of her thoughts. But then his presence was always a shock to her system.

She was convinced that she actually hated him, loathed the sight of him now, until he gave her a warm white smile as she joined them and something dark and hot twisted inside her and a dull, sweet ache coiled through the pit of her stomach.

With a supreme effort of will she met his smile with a frosty glare and sank down next to Janet, glad to take the weight off her suddenly shaky legs. She took a couple of deep breaths to calm herself and was able to speak.

'I'll leave you to make a decision on which designer you'd prefer to use. I'm going to have to hog the telephone and get things moving.' Her voice had begun to shake, so she said no more. Gideon's eyes were on her. She could feel them boring inside her head. She couldn't bear it!

She pushed back her chair, shaking her head as Dona held out the coffee-pot. She couldn't stay here a moment longer, knowing his clever eyes were watching the emotions she just knew were flickering over her face, assessing them, wondering, reaching conclusions...

'I need to fetch something from my room,' she invented thickly, and stumbled away, through the open French windows and back into the lovely cool tranquillity of the sitting room.

She put her slender hands convulsively over her

face, knocking her glasses awry. Her whole body was trembling, out of control, her legs barely able to hold her upright, let alone carry her up to her room.

She had believed she could hack it, but she obviously couldn't. She had far less will-power than she'd always thought. She couldn't stand the tension of being in his company a moment longer, couldn't stand the stress of wondering when his clever mind would ferret out her guilty secret. She only had to look at him, to feel his eyes on her, to hear his voice to want him with a desperation she would never have believed herself capable of feeling.

She had never been so overwrought and emotional in her life, and—

'What is it, Alice?' There was unmissable concern in the dark velvet voice, unmistakable tenderness in the way he took her hands and brought them down from her face, unhooking her skewed glasses from behind her ears and tucking them neatly into the breast pocket of her workmanlike blouse. 'Are you feeling unwell?'

His eyes swept comprehensively over her troubled features then probed deeply into her own, his hands warm and protective on her slight shoulders. Tears welled, stinging her eyes. And for a moment the temptation was unbearable.

The utter, impossible temptation of him. The insistent desire to weep her misery out against that pristine white shirt, to hear the pulsing beat of his heart, to wind her arms around his body and feel him holding her. Holding her close, and closer, giving her a fragment of time she could remember for ever...

She was fighting a battle with herself. A battle for

her self-respect and integrity. And she won. She dragged in a sharp breath and stepped away, her eyes glinting as she grated raggedly, 'Don't paw me around, Mr Rymer. Save that sort of tacky behaviour for the members of your wretched harem!'

CHAPTER FIVE

ALICE lifted her face to the sun, closed her eyes and breathed in the myriad scents of early summer: clean country air, newly mown grass and the heady perfume from the thousands of blossoms that foamed over the sides of Tossie's carefully tended containers, grouped in riotously lovely displays all around the courtyard.

Yesterday, when she'd been distraught enough, unguarded enough to shriek at Gideon, telling him to stop pawing her around because she wasn't one of his harem, she had known she'd gone much too far.

Especially when she'd seen the sudden dark glitter of his eyes, the cold anger that had compressed his sensual mouth into a bitter white line—the type of formidable line that would have had a hostile witness shaking in his shoes.

She had fully expected to be fired on the spot, and for that lapse of professionalism, she had belatedly realised, she would have deserved it.

But he had merely snapped, 'What makes you think you'd be admitted to that exclusive membership?' and then had stridden from the room, the rigid set of his magnificent shoulders showing his monumental contempt.

And she hadn't set eyes on him since.

If he'd returned to Rymer Court after that circuit dinner last night then she hadn't seen any sign of him. And that suited her just perfectly. With his absence she'd been gradually able to unwind, relax, to get on with the job she was here to do.

Yesterday afternoon and this morning she'd spent on the telephone, making arrangements, and with the arrival of the florist first thing this morning to discuss what would be needed everything was nicely in hand.

Except for the dress.

Janet, when pressed, had listlessly supposed Nico McGill's designs were OK. Alice had resisted the impulse to scream at such a lack of enthusiasm, and had retreated to her room to pick up the phone.

Nico had been delighted by the commission. He had tutted a bit over the lack of time at his disposal, but had accepted anyway, promising to fit in the initial consultation in the morning.

Alice had decided to stick around.

She had rallyingly explained to Janet that Nico would design a gown exclusively for her, something expressly created to make her look fantastic on her wedding day. But the bride's response had been lacklustre, so she would stay to make sure Janet showed up for that first, vital consultation.

Then she could make tracks, shake the dust of Rymer Court off her feet and begin to forget the shameful fact that she had come within a whisker of making a complete fool of herself over its unprincipled owner.

But in the meantime she would give herself a holiday. The long, glorious afternoon stretched ahead and she had nothing to do.

Janet had taken off again, destination unknown, and Gwen, after extolling the absent Gideon's virtues all through lunch—virtues Alice had decided, with jaundice, were all wishful thinking—had taken herself off upstairs.

So Alice had had a shower and washed her hair, and now it was spread to dry in glorious, curling burnished gold tendrils, reaching to just below her waist.

When she'd told Dona—while they were companionably clearing away the lunch things together—that she intended to grab herself a few hours of sunbathing, the warm-hearted housekeeper had offered her a loan of something more suitable than the neat skirts and blouses she'd brought with her.

Emerging from the shower, Alice had found a skimpy pair of lemon-yellow shorts and an even skimpier matching top laid out neatly on the bed. She'd put them on with some misgivings, but when she'd looked at herself in the glass she had almost believed she looked…well—a little bit sexy?

The tiny shorts and daringly cut bra-style top made her figure look positively pert. And her damp, luxuriant hair was quite spectacular when released from its confining braid.

Shaking her head and smiling wryly at her unprecedented moment of vanity, she had padded barefoot through the house, out through the deserted kitchen regions to lean, drowsily soaking up the sun, against the frame of the outer door.

'Nice to see you relaxing for once. Goodness—haven't you got wonderful hair? It's a stunning colour, and I bet you could sit on it!'

Alice opened her eyes and softly returned Tossie's generous smile. She was fixing a hose to a standpipe, preparing to water the containers, and Alice, smothering a yawn, pushed herself away from the support of the door frame and said, 'Thanks. It takes some looking after, but I've always been reluctant to cut it because it's the only good feature I have.'

'Rubbish!' Tossie scoffed. 'You look good all over from where I'm standing. Don't put yourself down!' She straightened, suddenly serious. 'How's it going? The wedding and stuff?'

'Fine.' Alice didn't really want to talk about it. She would rather forget it for an hour or so. The thought of the coming nuptials made her feel desolate. But she liked Tossie too much to brush her question aside. 'Most things are in hand, apart from the dress and the food. The caterers are sending sample menus…' Her voice trailed off, her throat tightening with misery. Dear God, she wished she'd never set eyes on Gideon Rymer!

'Do you ever wonder if you're wasting your time? If the wedding's going to take place?'

Alice gave her a quick, questioning look. Tossie wasn't joking, and it wasn't sour grapes; her lovely eyes were genuinely worried. 'What makes you say that?'

'Gut feeling.' Tossie shrugged her tanned shoulders, then stated more firmly, 'No, it's more than that. Look, don't think I'm speaking out of turn, but Gideon isn't in love with her.'

'How can you possibly know that?' Alice knew she sounded tart but she couldn't help it. Was Gideon having a secret affair with his gorgeous gardener? Or his housekeeper? Or both! Was that how Tossie knew what she herself had suspected all along?

'Because I know him. Me and Dona have talked it out. He's not in love with her, and that's a fact. He cares about her and there's a lot of affection—going back years. And he would have laid it on the line when he popped the question. He's not the man to say one thing and mean another; he's straight, he is!'

She was almost glaring now in her defence of her employer, and Alice envied her certainty, her staunch belief in the man's integrity.

'Anyway, that's the way it is,' Tossie said, calmer now but just as positive. 'And at first Jan seemed happy with the arrangement. Content, you know? Her and her mum moved in while work was being done at their place and everything ticked along nice and smooth. No mad passion, but then there wouldn't be. They acted like best friends, know what I mean?

'Then, a week or so back, Jan changed. She seemed to be avoiding him, kept taking herself off. Looking as if she'd lost a fiver and found a penny. And sometimes you catch him looking at her, sort of puzzled, as if he's wondering if he's doing the right thing. And I'll tell you something else for nothing. I don't know which one will do it, but one of them will call the whole thing off.'

'I hope you're wrong,' Alice lied. But what else could she say?

Janet deserved better than to be tied to a man who didn't love her, whose reasons for proposing in the first place had been decidedly suspect. And, despite Tossie's vehement defence, Alice was sure that the change in Janet had come about because she had discovered the man she had promised to marry wasn't in love with her. Nothing else could explain her obvious misery.

'And talking of long faces…' Tossie's voice went low. 'There's another one!'

A movement on the other side of the courtyard caught Alice's eye. A stocky young man with curly brown hair and a face that would have been ruggedly attractive if it hadn't been wearing such a dour expression was exiting one of the doors in the stable block.

'Who's that?'

'Will Gaunt, the land agent. Gideon hired him when he took over the running of the Manor lands and the home farm. He lives in the old gamekeeper's cottage. Nice chap, normally, but he's been acting like a bear with the proverbial just lately.'

They watched him stride over to a Land Rover and drive away. Tossie began watering and Alice, anxious to get away on her own and try to forget everything about the wedding for a short space of time, said, 'See you, then,' and headed for the gardens, determined to put Gideon right out of her head.

Just as she felt too hot to walk any longer, she came to a paved area in a secluded corner, complete with a padded swing seat with a shady awning, surrounded by sweeping beds of brilliant harlequin flowers. She took advantage, leaning back against the soft cushions, swinging slowly to and fro, her mind mercifully disengaging, thoughts drifting, her eyes slowly closing…

'I thought I was the only one who ever came here. Mind if I join you?'

The dipping of the swing seat, the rough velvet sound of his voice jolted her awake more effectively than a bucket of icy water. Her eyes snapped open, all her nerve-endings standing to attention as the all too familiar responses to him took control of her body.

'Don't you ever do any work?' She snapped the first defensive thought that came into her head, and in the split second of fraught silence that followed her outburst she chewed down savagely on her lower lip, sinkingly convinced that he'd be justifiably angry, ask her who the hell she thought she was speaking to and throw her off the job.

But he didn't. He gave her one of his more enigmatic smiles, maddening in its quality of teasing mystery, and leaned back in the seat, his head dipped slightly as he studied her troubled face.

'And I thought you looked so relaxed and at peace with yourself for once! But one word from me and you're spitting tacks. I wonder why?'

She didn't want him to wonder why! He might discover the awful truth! And she couldn't live with the humiliation of that. So she did her best to look and sound completely composed, even managing a tiny smile, a small, apologetic shrug.

'You startled me. I'm sorry. I thought you were in town, bringing tears to jurors' eyes.'

'Nope.' He picked up a strand of her tumbled hair and ran it slowly through his fingers. 'This is nice. I knew it would be glorious if it was ever allowed out of its strait-jacket.'

Oh, but his voice was a soft seduction in itself, and those appreciative glints in his blue, blue eyes made her heart flutter in her breast. All her precious, precarious control was slipping away! She felt herself tense, afraid to let herself relax because she couldn't trust herself not to fling herself at him, not to give in to the side of her nature she had never known she had.

And only slowly, very slowly, she exhaled her pent-up breath when the last of the strands of her captured hair slid through his fingers. Easing the tension a little, he clasped his hands behind his head and gazed out over the gardens.

'I recently finished a particularly gruelling case,' he told her. 'It followed hard on heels of another one that had been particularly long and involved. Hence the break. I'm free until after the wedding. How are things going in that department?'

'Fine.' It was a gross distortion of the truth, but again, what else could she say? It wasn't her place to point out that the wedding—if it took place at all, which Tossie at least seemed to doubt—would be nothing but a prelude to disaster.

He would be marrying for all the wrong reasons, plus a chunk of valuable property, and Janet must have recently discovered the truth—that he didn't love her at all—which was why she was too miserable to take an interest in the great day. She didn't even care about what kind of dress she would wear when she walked up the aisle to make her vows.

'Good.'

Not a whole load of enthusiasm there either. But then there wouldn't be. Alice risked a sideways glance.

His eyes were closed now, those ridiculously long black lashes almost touching his hard, jutting cheekbones. So her eyes were free to roam unobserved, uncontrolled, unwillingly yet lovingly following the broad, hard line of his shoulders, the lean, muscular body, the long, long legs. All casually packaged in a sleeveless olive-green T-shirt and toning cotton twill trousers.

Then his eyes flew open, the startling, glittering blue still having the power to surprise, to mesmerise, to make her feel that she was all he wanted to see. They locked precisely with hers and she looked away quickly, her blood leaping wildly through her veins.

'I'll be leaving tomorrow, as soon as the designer has consulted with Janet,' she said in a flurried rush. 'So I must get on. I'll leave you in peace.'

'Such a hurry!'

She was already unsteadily on her feet, but he circled her wrist with his thumb and forefinger, his eyes making a detailed inventory of her scantily clad body. She subsided unresistingly back on the cushions, because the open caress of his eyes sucked the strength from her body.

Too late, she wished the things Dona had lent her were much less revealing. Without her neat office clothes, her tidy no-nonsense braid, she felt unprotected, achingly vulnerable.

And she was shaking inside. She could feel the tiny tremors invading every inch of her body. So close to him, so alone with him, she was incapable of behaving like a rational human being.

Her reaction to him disgusted her. But she couldn't change it. She had tried and she'd failed, and, even though the unpleasant facts were staring her in the face, he still had the power to bewitch her.

All his adult life he would have been used to seeing women falling at his feet, their eyes devouring him, begging him to notice them. So used to being fawned over, he would have come to expect it, sweeping those mesmerising eyes over what was on offer, taking his pick, using and discarding. That would be his way.

A cold-blooded man, despite that smouldering, simmering sexuality. Cold enough to consider marrying for financial gain.

And because she was possibly the one woman who hadn't sought his company, the one who tried to leave it as soon as she possibly could, he was intrigued. Not knowing the reason, he was setting out to prove to himself that he could bring her under his spell.

It was an assumption, but surely not a wild one? Why else should he want her to stay, to keep her here with him?

At least, she tried to console herself, he couldn't have yet realised that as far as spells went she was well and truly under his. Because if he knew that he would have proved his point and would lose all interest. He would be able to look at her and not even see her. He certainly wouldn't be physically preventing her from walking away, and that meant he hadn't guessed the way he made her feel.

'Stay a while. Keep me company.'

'Some of us need to work at keeping up with the pack,' she pointed out, trying to drag her captured hand away from his long, manacling fingers, but failing.

'And where's the point in that, if you lose the art of appreciating everything around you? Why deny yourself the time to simply stand and stare, to learn about things, about people?'

The warm curl of amusement in his voice made her suck in her breath. He was mocking her for being the woman she was. Heat raged through her bloodstream, colouring her face as his voice flooded her with honey-sweet waves. You've been here—what? A couple of days? And yet I know next to nothing about you. And I want to. I want to know what makes you tick.'

'Why?' Her voice sounded rough. So that was his line, was it? Let's get to know each other. As a prelude to what?

'You intrigue me.'

He was shooting a line. Well, she knew that. But knowing it didn't stop a wicked, forbidden tremor of excitement sweeping through her body.

Agitatedly, her free hand went up to worry at the corner of her mouth. He shouldn't be holding her hand, talking to her this way. He was engaged to poor Janet. She shouldn't be letting it happen. She should be snatching her hand away, standing up, marching away. Telling him to keep his smooth tongue still in his mouth.

She didn't know where all her self-respect had gone.

He reached for her other hand, the agitated one, caught it, held it. Smiled.

Alice struggled to regroup her tattered defences and fought back. 'Ours is a purely business relationship. Impersonal. Terminated as soon as I've finished here.'

'Quite. Let's take that as a jumping-off point, shall we? Tell me how you came to start your own business, make such a success of it.'

She had managed to extricate her hands, and he

hadn't fought to hold onto them. Which should have left her mightily relieved, but hadn't because he had shifted his long legs slightly, his body turned to hers, and one of his arms had somehow draped itself along the back of the seat behind her.

But if she hadn't got the moral strength, the will-power to walk away—which sadly she hadn't—then her business, which was the most important thing in her life, and a completely impersonal subject, was an OK topic to launch out on.

She would probably bore him to tears, and he'd be reduced to inventing a phone call he absolutely had to make in order to shut her up and get away.

And that would be fine by her. Perfect. It would take the pressure off. The pressure of being cocooned with him in this secluded place. The pressure of not allowing him to get the faintest intimation of the ap-palling way he affected her.

'So?' he insisted gently. 'How did you begin? What gave you the idea?'

That was easy. Despite herself, she smiled.

'I have three very beautiful sisters, older than me. Arabella, Angel and Amaryllis. By the time I came along, Ma must have run out of exotic names begin-ning with A—goodness only knows why she got fix-ated on that letter of the alphabet, but she did—so she gave up on the striking and named me plain Alice. Either that or she could see into the future, to the spots on my face, braces on my teeth, specs on the end of my nose, and decided something plain would be more fitting.'

Much more relaxed now, she crossed one leg over the other, clasping her hands around her knee, leaning forward, unaware that the unconscious pose deepened her cleavage. Unaware of the sudden sobering of his eyes, the attentive way he was looking at her.

'Anyway, as my sisters had only one goal in life, to marry and marry well—which wasn't difficult, considering the way they look—I was dragooned into helping Ma organise three weddings, each one huger and splashier than the last. My sisters have always been a competitive bunch!'

She gave him a sideways smile, discovering how easy it was to talk to him. It was like talking to an old and valued friend, someone who would always be on your side, no matter what.

'I was being a dutiful if unwilling brides-maid at Angel's wedding—the last of the three to tie the knot—when I had this flash of inspiration.'

She turned her head, grinning openly at him now because she loved talking about her work, was proud of the way she had made it happen. She stabbed the spectacles which had the habit of slithering down when she was talking back up her nose.

'I suddenly knew where my future lay—not in marriage, that was for sure, but in organising it for other people and being paid handsomely for doing it! Having been Ma's right hand through three spectacular weddings there wasn't a lot to learn, apart from the business side of it.'

'You weren't interested in marriage.' His eyes scanned her animated features. 'Most girls are, sooner or later.'

'No way.' She was definite about that. 'When I was younger, growing up, no one noticed me when my sisters were around. They were—still are—exquisite.

I used to let it get to me until I got my head together and decided what I wanted out of life.'

'Which is?'

'Independence. To achieve something I can be proud of. Look at it this way—when each of my sisters reached the age of eighteen, Dad, who's a retired banker and likes to indulge his womenfolk, splashed out. Whatever we wanted, when our turn came, we could have. Jewellery, complete designer outfits, snappy sports cars were favourite—they increased their prospects of attracting the right kind of attention, you see. I asked for the capital to start Hearts and Flowers. There's the difference.

'I'd already done a gruelling course in business studies, and it was tough going to begin with, getting the clients. But it's coming good now and I've never regretted it, especially as none of my sisters seem really contented. Arabella in particular. Her husband was on the point of divorcing her not so long ago.'

The words were bubbling out of her. She seemed unable to stop them. There was something about this man that invited openness. A gift that must be worth its weight in gold in the law profession.

'She'd been bored, been seeing another man. She told me it was just a silly fling, and couldn't understand why Ben—he's her husband—was making such a fuss. I told her to get her priorities right and make up her mind about what she did want—a series of silly flings or a decent, stable marriage to a decent, stable man.'

'Ah.' Gideon ran a fingertip lightly down the length of her arm and something inside her trembled softly;

her babbling confidences remained muted in her throat. 'They're all the same, Alice.'

She moistened her lips with the tip of her tongue and hoped against hope that her voice would emerge normally, would not betray her, tell him how light-headed the soft drift of his finger against her naked flesh had made her feel.

'What? What are all the same?' she managed at last, and he wasn't smiling now.

'Beautiful women. Especially when they're wives.'

She looked at him uncertainly, her eyes clouding as she remembered just who she'd been chattering to for the last half an hour. And she understood now, or was fairly certain she did.

He might adore beautiful women—one only had to look at his so-called harem, observe the way he was with them to know that—but he wouldn't trust them as far as he could throw them.

Because of what his mother had done to him and his father.

And because of that deep-seated distrust he was marrying Janet because she was plain, and safe—highly unlikely to stray. And, to make matters even better, she was a considerable heiress.

Held tightly within that understanding was a warm core of compassion. The knowledge that his past, and the influence of the people in his life when he had been young—in his case his embittered father—reached out to affect his present, just as hers did, made her feel close to him, really close to him.

Their eyes held, locked together in long moments of growing understanding. It was as if, Alice thought with a sigh of stolen contentment, they were word-lessly sharing secrets. Bonding.

And then the soft, dangerous smile was back in his eyes, gently curving that all too sensual male mouth, and the sober, inexplicably poignant moment was broken, because he lifted her spectacles off her nose and murmured, 'Know something, Alice? Whatever you may have been led to believe, you are beautiful. Very.'

And he kissed her.

CHAPTER SIX

IT WAS the sweetest thing Alice had ever known—unimaginable in her limited experience. Exquisite sensations swept her upwards, spiralling giddily onto an unexplored plane of colour and light and dizzy, exploding stars.

The stroke of Gideon's lips against hers was like the breathtaking discovery of heaven, the honey-sweet answer to the riddle of the universe, and as his hands gently cupped her face, his long fingers threading into the glorious riot of her hair, her lips parted instinctively, willingly, greedily at the infinitely sensual pressure of his.

Small mews of pleasure rippled in her throat, and then a gasp of intense, almost shocked excitement as she felt the flimsy borrowed covering tighten over her shamelessly peaking breasts. Her hands went to his wide, angular shoulders; she couldn't stop them any more than she could prevent her fingers digging into the hard muscle, pulling him closer, needing him to be closer, so very much closer, because only the physical storm of his body against hers could ease this heated, near painful pleasure, turn it to fiery ecstasy.

Then she felt the slight stiffening of his body, the timeless, silent pause when everything—the beats of the heart, the mechanism of breathing—when life itself seemed suspended on the knife-edge of a momentous decision. And then, just as her heart began to beat again, racing, tumbling about beneath her aching breasts, he put her away from him, his hands gentle but determined on her shoulders.

For a moment her eyes couldn't focus. She was overwhelmed by the loss of rapture, the painful beginnings of guilt, and then she saw the tight jerk of a muscle at the side of his hard jaw, the leaching of life from his eyes, the bleakness, and believed he shared her anguish, the guilty knowledge that this shouldn't have happened.

But she knew she was mistaken. Blindly, stupidly, hopelessly so. Because she saw the kindness in his eyes now, heard the lacing of laughter in his caring voice as he popped her spectacles back on her nose.

She felt the blood drain from her face. Her nerves were shot to pieces. He had, in his own inimitable way, simply been telling her something.

And he proved her right when he drawled, 'You're a delectable little creature, Alice. Eminently kissable. Just because you believed your sisters got all the best gifts from the christening party Good Fairy, leaving nothing over for you, there was no need to give up, hide behind a load of prickly defences and passion-killer clothes.' He took her hands, uncurled the clenched fingers and stroked them gently. 'You are you. Unique and special. And lovely. Don't let anyone, ever, tell you differently. And don't ever forget it.'

She was trying not to cry. Trying very hard. Trying to find a snippy comeback, something to put him in his place. But suddenly she knew she couldn't be like that, not with him, not ever again.

He had charmed his way right through her de-

fences, blown every last one of them away. She was
shaking inside, still shellshocked by what he had
made her feel. But her precious common sense put in
a belated appearance, and she knew she couldn't just
sit there, gazing at him with misty eyes.

She couldn't allow him to know that the effect of
that kiss, for her at least, had been momentous. So
she removed her hands gently from his. No more
snatching and snapping.

'I must go,' she told him as steadily as she could.
'I thought I might drive into Wantage this afternoon
as there's nothing useful I can do around here until
the morning.' She hadn't thought of going anywhere,
not until right this minute, but it served its purpose
because he didn't try to detain her this time as she
sprang to her feet.

He didn't reply and she looked at him uncertainly.
He was leaning back now, his eyes closed, and she
saw lines of strain on his features, an indication of
stress that was totally new in her experience of him.

Fleetingly, she wondered if she should say something. Anything. Something chirpy like, Well, see you
at dinner, then! simply to let him know there were no
hard feelings, that one little kiss was nothing to worry
over.

But she decided against it because he certainly
wouldn't be worrying over an unimpassioned kiss,
given in friendship to make a point. And she slipped
away, making for the house, not even trying to stop
the tears now. She was weeping for something momentarily glimpsed, something precious, something
lost. Surely she was entitled?

She made it to her room without seeing a soul,

dampened her face, caught her hair into the nape of her neck with an elastic band and changed into the suddenly depressingly dowdy skirt and blouse.

She knew she should be feeling as guilty as hell over what had happened. She had arrived at Rymer Court to do her best for the bride-to-be, to use her considerable organising talents to effect an unforgettable and perfect wedding day for the happy couple. And she had ended up wanting the groom—wanting him with a hunger that drove everything else out of her head.

Even guilt.

She couldn't harm Janet. She had taken nothing away from her because that kiss, for him, had been nothing. He probably regarded kissing as a harmless little hobby, something to be openly and honestly enjoyed, like inhaling the fragrance of a rose or watching a sunset.

The only person to be harmed was herself. As her mother would have said, there would be tears before bedtime! She had only herself to blame for the state she was in. She was being justly punished because a woman of her age had no right to indulge in juvenile infatuation.

And that was all it could be. She would not let herself admit to it being anything else. And as for that kiss, well, she would make it work for her, not against her. Look at it logically.

He had listened to her bleating on about her gorgeous sisters and had cleverly—well, that went without saying, didn't it?—delved right to the bottom of her hang-ups and kissed her. Very kindly.

There had been nothing dark or lustful about it;

he'd been trying to show her, to actually demonstrate, that she had nothing to be ashamed of in the looks department, that she could, and should, hold her own. That she was kissable...

Looked at in that light, his kiss had been a gift, offering her a new confidence if she had the wits to take it, a different type of belief in herself. And for that she had to feel grateful. Not guilty. She had taken nothing from Janet.

And for what was left of the afternoon she was going to indulge her new self, because that might make it real to her and not merely something dreamed up in self-defence. In time she would be able to look back on this fraught period of her life, her senseless infatuation, with gratitude to him for opening her eyes to her own physical potential—and a wry smile for her own gullibility.

Her car had been parked in part of the extensive stable block, and she was backing it out when Tossie appeared, trundling a loaded barrow. Alice trod on the brakes and cut the engine when Tossie leaned through the open driver's-side window and pushed a strand of blonde hair back from her face with a heavy-duty-gloved hand.

'Did you see Gideon? He came back and was looking for you. I told him you'd last been seen heading for the gardens. Did he find you?'

'He did.'

Alice, vividly recalling what had happened, willed herself not to blush. But looking for her? For what reason? He had barely mentioned the forthcoming wedding, the work he was paying her so handsomely to do. He had merely asked offhandedly how things were going and had then gone on to ask her to keep him company, tell him something about herself.

Had he really come looking for her because he'd wanted to spend time with her? Wanted to get to know her better?

Unlikely as that seemed, she still felt her face go pink, and it went positively scarlet when Tossie, happy to chat a while, leaned her arms on the window-frame and grinned at her.

'Lucky you! Most men would give their pension funds to have Gideon Rymer hunt them down!'

'Including you?' Alice couldn't resist it. The leggy blonde gardener was so utterly lovely, and Gideon's reaction to her—and Dona—was relaxed, intimate and definitely appreciative. No one would blame Tossie for yearning. 'Are you one of his groupies?'

'Groupies? Nah!' Tossie's big blue eyes sparkled with laughter. 'Me and Dona just love him for what he is.'

Alice got back to Rymer Court at the far end of the afternoon, hot, sweaty and headachy after her frantic dash around the shops. She clutched an armful of carrier bags—proof of her indulgence of the new self, the possibilities that Gideon, with that gentle kiss, those few kind words, had opened up in front of her.

So she'd never set the world aflame with her dazzling appearance, but she sure as heck wouldn't let herself smother what attributes she did have under dowdy—what had Gideon called them?—passion-killer clothes. It was almost as if she'd been unconsciously punishing herself for not being as beautiful as her sisters.

She met Gwen coming down the stairs as she was rushing up.

'Where's Janet? Has she been with you?'

'No, she went out directly after lunch. She's not needed until the designer comes in the morning.' The wrong thing to have said, Alice thought as she witnessed the older woman actually wringing her hands. She hadn't thought people really did that.

'Not needed? Of course she's needed.' The worry line between her eyes deepened. 'Gideon's been back for hours. My daughter's place should be here, with him. Not... Well, the dear boy will begin to think—'

Here was someone else who was puzzled by the engaged couple's odd behaviour. Only in Gwen's case it was more like acute anxiety. 'Perhaps she went over to the Manor,' Alice suggested gently. 'I believe she and Mr Rymer are keen to see the work completed before the wedding.'

It was hard to mention the wedding and sound as if her only interest was professional when everything inside her cried out against it happening at all. But Gwen's distress was too great to let her detect emotional discord in someone else.

'No. I went there. The decorators said they hadn't seen her. Oh, if only dear Rose were here—she'd know what to do!'

'Well, she can't have got lost. She'll come home when she's hungry!' She tried to make a joke of it, willing the other woman to lighten up, but Gwen wasn't going to do any such thing and continued on her way downstairs without saying another word.

Alice watched her. Wondering. She thought she

knew why Janet was miserable. She had discovered that the man she had promised to marry, the man she loved, didn't love her. She was entitled to be miserable.

Had she confided in her mother? Was Gwen having problems with that? Was she afraid her mousy little daughter might throw away her golden opportunity to become the wife of Gideon the Wonderful? Gwen, in common with everyone else around here, believed the earth revolved around him.

Determinedly, she pushed the whole sorry tangle out of her mind. They would have to sort themselves out. By this time tomorrow she would be back in London, her personal involvement finished. She would pass the paperwork, the telephoned finalising of the arrangements over to her assistant. And she would occupy her mind, right now, with the decision of what to wear this evening.

The sunflower-yellow shift, or the blue silk trousers and matching top?

The shift. Yes, definitely the shift. It had made her look surprisingly elegant when she'd tried it on.

Stuffing her hair into a shower cap, she changed her mind, and an hour later went down to find the others wearing a dress of fine diaphanous cotton with a smudgy design of soft rose and faded green flowers on a warm cream background. The full skirt whispered seductively around her legs and the sleeveless V-necked bodice lovingly moulded itself to her pert breasts, emphasising her tiny waist.

She hadn't bothered to braid her hair, had just given it a thorough brushing and left it as it was, dropping like a gold silk curtain down to her waist.

To counteract the youthful appearance of her hair she wore her new, outrageously expensive Italian sandals—very high heels and a cat's-cradle of narrow straps—and she had used much more eye make-up than she usually bothered with to offset the owly glasses.

She found the others, as expected at this time of the evening, on the terrace, sitting around the lavishly spread table. Her eyes went unstoppably, instinctively to Gideon. He was wearing a dark-coloured silk shirt, open at the neck, and off-white cotton chinos. He looked fantastic.

He got to his feet with his usual lazy grace, his narrowed eyes taking in every detail of her appearance, the lowered fringe of thick dark lashes not quite hiding the appreciative glitter.

Alice's stupidly responsive heart gave a quicksilver leap, her breath shivering in her lungs as his eyes slid back up her slender body and fastened intently on her slightly parted lips.

Was he remembering how he'd kissed her? Recalling her eager response? Oh, she mustn't let herself think things like that—dangerous, yearning thoughts. But was that why the two of them seemed locked into another dimension, another plane, where only the two of them existed?

Something inside her twisted over, sharp and vital and stingingly sweet. And there was nothing she could do about it. Her responses to this man were beyond her control. She wished he would stop looking at her, his unreadable eyes still heart-stoppingly focused on her mouth, the dark and dangerous spell unbreakable.

The tip of her tongue nervously laved her lips, and his eyes flicked up and locked with hers.

She couldn't look away, couldn't move. Her eyes widened as she registered the grimly savage line of his mouth, and his brows bunched above his suddenly hard, dark eyes as he reached for a chair and pulled it away from the table for her, then retook his own seat.

Alice sat quickly, unsure of herself, of what had happened—because something *had* happened, silently, contained in a look. A long and searching look that had made everything change. She was confused. But not for long.

'Help yourself,' Janet said, sounding edgy. 'We don't stand on ceremony.'

Gwen, obviously trying to act as if everything was coming up roses, was chattering about the coming wedding. She wanted to be brought up to date on everything that had been put in hand so far, as if by talking about it she would ensure that it happened.

Alice, trying to give reassuringly enthusiastic answers, emerged from her own confusion.

He obviously approved of her altered appearance, but had quickly absorbed the ramifications and had got the wrong end of the stick. He would have been remembering his words of advice, the way he'd demonstrated her potential as a woman with a teasing kiss, and her fevered, immediate response.

He believed she'd prettied herself up, made herself attractive in order to lure him into giving her more of the same!

It couldn't be further from the truth. She hadn't splashed out on new, ultra-feminine clothes to please him. She'd done it for herself, because his demonstration had made her see herself in a new light. But nothing else could explain that frown, that hard, dark look, the austere grimness in the angry slash of his mouth.

The humiliation was intense.

Trying to keep up with Gwen's questions, she helped herself to some salad from the lavish spread Dona had provided, and Gideon reached over and filled her wineglass. She glanced up and met his eyes, saw him look quickly away, as if he found the sight of her distasteful. Misery swept over her in icy waves.

Her suspicions were confirmed. He *did* believe she'd read more into that innocuous kiss than had been there.

His very silence was warning her not to be so presumptuous. The type of woman who would arouse his sexual interest would be vastly different from her. Sophisticated, polished, very experienced. She recalled the telephone numbers kept in his secret black book. For use when he grew bored with marriage to a woman he didn't love.

And what did his assumptions say of her integrity? That she was willing—provided her new, less frigid appearance could tempt him into it—to embark on a sordid, furtive affair?

If he privately believed that, he was way off the mark! She would never do such a thing! True, she was having trouble with her sudden rush of hormones, her ridiculous infatuation. But she was working on it. And tomorrow she would be gone, out of sight would be out of mind and she could forget all about it. And get on with her life.

'I'll get going.' Janet had barely touched her food, and had been as silent as the brooding Gideon.

'Where to?' Gwen stopped discussing menus for the reception and looked sharply at her daughter.

Janet pushed her chair back from the table and answered quickly, 'Home. I thought I'd told you. I want to measure up for new curtains before the light goes. We can't re-hang the old ones; they're threadbare.'

Any further discussion on the subject was forestalled when Dona appeared briefly.

'Telephone for you, Gwen. In the study.' She beamed at them all. 'I'll bring coffee out in a few minutes.'

She disappeared and Gwen got to her feet, excusing herself.

'I'll make tracks, then,' said Janet. 'Don't worry if I'm late. I want to get it all sorted out tonight.' She sounded breathless, as if she'd already spent hours rushing around, instead of doing nothing more strenuous than pushing a spoonful of tomato-coated pasta around her plate.

Alice risked a glance at Gideon, wondering if he would accompany his future wife. But he made no move, his expression on the grim side of abstracted.

All he asked was, 'Are you taking the car?'

Already at the French windows, Janet turned, shaking her head. 'I thought I'd walk across the fields. It's just as quick as taking the car the long way round by road. Quicker.' Then, meeting his sudden frown, she reassured him hastily, 'If I get a move on I'll be back before dark. I'll take a torch, just in case.'

And she was gone, leaving a tense silence behind

her, until Gideon said, without inflexion, 'Let me give you some more wine.'

He reached for her empty glass at the moment she put out a hand to cover it. She didn't want any more alcohol. Her head was already spinning from the glassful she'd recklessly swallowed earlier.

She dragged in a sharp breath as his fingers touched hers, and for a split second her whole body tensed as shock waves of sensation flooded fiercely, hotly and sweetly through her system. Then, instinctively, defensively, she snatched her hand away at the precise moment of his own sudden, impulsive withdrawal and the glass fell, shattering against the salad bowl.

'I'm sorry—' Alice clamped her trembling lips together, her face pale with shock. Something had happened, something far more traumatic than the clumsy accident with the glass.

She didn't know what it was, not precisely, but she could see the aftermath of it in the expressionless stab of his eyes, in the hard white line of his mouth as he pushed back his chair and snapped to his feet, could hear it in the harsh precision of his voice.

'Leave it. Dona will deal with it. If you'll excuse me, I have work to do.'

He couldn't leave her company quickly enough. He didn't even look at her. Perhaps he couldn't bear to, because distaste was written in every line of his face.

His voice was cold, rimmed with ice, as he suggested, 'Perhaps you could bring yourself to do the same? Time's pressing. The wedding is very close. Aren't there still things for you to organise? Or am I paying you a vast amount of money to go sunbathing, shopping and generally laze around?'

CHAPTER SEVEN

HE HAD gone, leaving Alice staring sightlessly into space, her eyes brimming with sudden, burning tears.

Her hands clenched in her lap, her nails digging painfully into her palms. How dared Gideon imply she was taking his damned money under false pretences? How dared he?

He was the one who had mockingly taunted her for being the type of career-crazy woman who had to be hard at work before she could justify the air she breathed. He was the one who had fully expected her to be here at Rymer for a couple of weeks, who had teased her, telling her to learn to mix business with pleasure, adding that she might even grow to like it!

So how dared the wretched man turn round after only a couple of days or so and unfairly accuse her of swinging the lead, lazing around at his expense?

She had done her level best, working hard with very little co-operation from anyone. She was only still here now because she had to sit in on the initial consultation between Janet and Nico tomorrow.

But worse than the justifiable anger, far, far worse, was the hurt and humiliation. It flayed her, cutting her to pieces, leaving her shivering, full of pain.

His complete volte-face had to be a direct result of that gentle kiss, her stupid reaction to it and his unreasonable assumptions.

He really thought she'd dressed herself up to get

his attention—more of it, more kisses. And he was putting her down, firmly in her place. He might just as well have come straight out with it: Take you for a bit on the side? In your dreams, lady!

A sob threatened to choke her, but she swallowed it back angrily, snatching at her glasses and scrubbing at her eyes with a soft paper napkin.

She hated him. She hated his humiliating assumptions! Why she had ever thought herself infatuated with him she couldn't imagine. She had been a stupid fluff-head—like a schoolgirl with more hormones than common sense!

But at least she was cured. Well and truly over it.

Putting her glasses back on, she stood up from the table just as Dona appeared with the coffee-tray and a dustpan and brush.

'Oh, don't go!' She slid the tray onto the end of the table, the silver coffee-pot turned to rosy pink by the slanting rays of the warm evening sun. 'I got delayed. So we'll have coffee together as everyone else seems to have deserted you.'

She was already pouring out, and Alice sank down on her chair again. She wasn't in the mood for company but she didn't want to appear rude. It wasn't the housekeeper's fault that her employer was a louse!

Dona passed her a cup of coffee and peered at the mess of broken glass.

'I'll see to that in a minute.' She hitched up a chair. 'I don't know what's come over everyone,' she confided. 'First Janet starts going around with a long face, then her mother begins to act all strange—babbling about the wedding one minute and then, when she thinks no one's looking, going around with her face on the floor, acting like she's had a bill for a thousand pounds and she's only got sixpence in the bank! And now Gideon!'

She rolled her dark eyes expressively, oblivious of her companion's tight features. 'When he came to tell me there'd been an accident with a glass he had a face on him that would have frozen a volcano! He's never like that. Something or someone must have got him in a rage!'

Alice shuddered. She knew who that someone was. And the something was the distasteful matter—as he saw it—of being chased by a lustful wedding organiser!

'Well, whatever—or whoever—it can't be because he's had a spat with his fiancée.' Dona had finished her coffee and was inspecting the shards of glass. 'Better get rid of this. No, Gideon and Janet—friends for years. It's fairly common knowledge that there's no passion involved. It's going to be one of those comfy marriages. You know, no passion—so a difference of opinion wouldn't have left him in a black rage—but lots of liking, affection, respect, and being ever so polite to each other at all times.'

And property, Alice added in her head. Don't forget the property!

She hated him even more. Hated him so much that her hands were shaking as she helped Dona clear the table, leaving her a clean sweep with the dustpan and brush.

'Perhaps it's all down to nerves,' Dona suggested. 'Though I'd have said there was nothing Gideon couldn't handle. I guess we'll all be glad when the wedding's over and the atmosphere's back to normal.'

Alice could only say Amen to that and excuse herself. She was too churned up to go into the bookroom and watch television. Walking aimlessly held little appeal. But the thought of going to bed, tossing and turning, held even less.

Her walk needn't be aimless, she decided as she gazed frustratedly around her room. She changed into sensible shoes. She could walk over to meet Janet on her way back. Why not? Even if she couldn't find her way across the fields the exercise would calm her mind, help her to sleep. And tomorrow she would be out of here, would stop thinking about Gideon Rymer and think about her work, take up her neglected social life.

She set off, cutting across the lawns and finding the track through the trees where Gideon had said he ran each morning. She imagined his tanned and splendid physique...

She reached a field gate and noted the well-trodden track slanting obliquely across the cropped green grass. Clambering over the gate, she followed it. The grazing sheep didn't bother to scatter; midges danced low in the air.

From then on it was easy, because this was obviously the short cut between Janet's home and Gideon's, and ten minutes later she was standing on the brow of a rounded hill looking down on the mellow stone Manor House, which was cosily surrounded by fertile pastureland and acres of broad-leafed woodland that ran down to the little river which wound its way along the valley floor.

An enviable property indeed. A fair exchange for a life with a woman he didn't love?

The track joined the rutted drive near one of the gable ends, and although the evening light was fading now there were no lights that Alice could see—at least not on this side of the house.

There were none on the other either, although one of the side doors lay open. There was no way she could have missed the other girl on the way over here, and Janet wouldn't have left the house open like this, so Alice decided to go in and find her.

She went through the door and found herself in a side hall smelling of fresh plaster and sawdust. There were four panelled doors and what looked like a corridor that led to another, larger hall. It would take ages to search the rambling property, and the light was going fast.

She was about to call out, when the still, dusky silence was broken suddenly by the sound of weeping. Ragged, distraught, helpless weeping.

Janet. Obviously desperately unhappy and alone.

Alice traced the source of the sound to the room immediately on her right and pushed on the door, her heart clenching in sympathy for the other woman's bitter distress, guessing the reason for it. It had to be down to the heartless brute she was about to marry.

'Janet?' She stepped over the threshold, calling out, then could have bitten her tongue out of her head because Janet wasn't alone. She was held in a passionate embrace, the falling tears being frenziedly kissed from her face, and the man who was doing the kissing wasn't Gideon.

For a moment the couple were frozen, the air turbulent with wild emotion. And then they turned, as one, to look at her. Janet's face was ashen, streaked

with tears, Will Gaunt's grim with an anguish that
came from deep within the heart.

Gideon's land agent.

'I'm sorry,' Alice muttered thickly, hurriedly stepping back out of the room, deeply embarrassed for
herself and for them, then gathered herself and scurried back the way she had come. She hadn't covered
more than a dozen yards when she heard Janet call
her name.

She turned slowly, reluctantly. She didn't want to
get involved. Her fingers went to her temples, as if to
contain a thousand and one disjointed, confusing
thoughts. Janet was hugging her arms around her
body, her unremarkable features ravaged by weeping.

'Please— Alice, please don't—' she began raggedly, then covered her face with her hands, an oddly
touching, childish gesture that made Alice want to
comfort her, tell her everything was all right.

But it wasn't all right. She hadn't known Janet
Cresswell long, but long enough to suspect that she
wasn't the type to opt for a sophisticated, open-style
marriage, where both partners were free to take a
string of lovers provided they were discreet about it.

She bit her lip as she watched the other girl struggle
for control. How could she be engaged to marry
Gideon and even *see* another man?

'Please, Alice, don't say anything to Gideon, or
anyone, about—about what you saw!' Janet pleaded
brokenly. 'I can't explain now, but I will. I promise!'

'What you do and who you do it with is not my
concern,' she answered stiffly, suddenly angry, bit-
terly angry. 'I'm here to organise your wedding day,
that is all. Not to make moral judgements.'

Turning on her heel, she walked away, hating them all. Janet for taking her sympathies and turning them into disgust, for having a sneaky affair with her future husband's employee, for weeping and wailing because she'd been found out and dragging her, Alice Rampton, into the sordid intrigue by begging her to say nothing.

And Gideon for involving her too. For making her want him, making her hate him, for the humiliation he'd so coldly dished out.

As she gained the brow of the hill she decided to throw the commission back in Gideon's face, tell him to find someone else to organise his farce of a wedding.

She didn't want to have anything to do with it—a wedding between two people who probably deserved each other. Gideon was marrying for mercenary reasons, and probably looking forward to a life of cheating on a wife who was already cheating on him!

She would have nothing to do with a wedding that would make an evil mockery of the vows that would be made in church!

She would pack her bags and leave tonight. She couldn't wait to get back to sanity and normality!

Pausing to catch her breath as she crested the hill, she scanned the pastureland she would have to cross with a sinking heart.

It was almost dark now, and, while crossing the fields out in the open would be no real problem, finding the track and keeping to it through the densely planted belt of trees would.

She didn't have a torch. She had expected to be walking back with the perfidious Janet, who had. But at least Janet's long and puzzling absences were explained, as well as her lack of any real interest in the wedding arrangements. She had been sneaking off to be with her lover, her mind too full of him to allow space for anything as dull as her wedding day!

She was sick of the lot of them!

Grinding her teeth, she clambered over the field gate and trudged on, wary of wasting what little light there was.

Darkness had well and truly closed in when she reached the trees and began to search for the track. She had almost given up hope of ever finding it, was beginning to worry that she'd still be blundering about in the morning, not securely back in her own little home where she desperately wanted to be, comfortless and soulless though it undeniably was.

When she saw the beam of light approaching through the trees, many yards to the right of where she had been futilely poking around, her initial reaction was one of enormous relief.

She began to move towards it. At least there was someone about who would be able to put her on the right track. But her relief turned to bitter dismay as some sixth sense told her that this was Gideon.

She had never wanted to have to see him again, not after he'd made her feel so humiliated. She couldn't cope with the raw emotions he brought to life within her.

Sagging against the bole of a tree, she struggled to catch her breath, to steady her wild heartbeats. She was having a panic attack!

'What the hell...?' Torchlight shone mercilessly into her eyes. 'What are you doing out here?'

She didn't know what to say. I'm lost in the dark because I thought I'd be coming back with Janet, only she's otherwise occupied with your land agent, wouldn't go down too well, and, much as she despised what was going on, she couldn't bring herself to betray the other girl.

Besides, now she came to think of it, Janet had been crying, obviously deeply distressed, before she knew her guilty secret had been discovered.

She shook her head, her eyes screwed up because the light was hurting them, and, thankfully, he took the hint and lowered the hand that held the torch. He couldn't see her face as she made the only response she could think of.

'The same as you, I suppose.'

'I doubt it. I'm on my way to meet Janet.' His tone was dry, unamused. 'She's late and I'm restless.'

Alice's mouth went dry. Goodness only knew what he'd find back at the Manor. And Janet had begged her not to betray her, had promised to explain. As if anything could explain away the scene she'd walked in on. But, remembering the deep unhappiness on that ordinary little face, Alice stated, 'Then I'll come with you.'

She didn't want to go anywhere with him, didn't want to see him, speak to him. But there really was no alternative.

'No.' His response was immediate, curt and cold, and her face crawled with humiliated colour.

'Don't worry,' she snapped back. 'I won't try to ravish you under a bush! You're perfectly safe, so give your massive ego a rest, why don't you? I have to go with you because you have a torch. I can't see a damn thing,' she stated snippily. 'I meant to get back before dark, but I got lost. Do you really think I'd hang onto your company if I had any option?'

So he could let that sink into his insufferably conceited head, and if she went with him at least she could do something. Make a noise—talk at the top of her voice as they approached the house. It was all she could do.

'Have the bloody torch!' He thrust it at her. 'I don't need it and Jan will have her own.' The tone of his voice told her that he didn't want her company at any price. That despite what she'd said he didn't believe she wasn't lusting after his body, panting for the opportunity to get her hands on him.

Tears of rage and humiliation stung her eyes, and rage came out on top, making her say, 'I'll have to come with you. I can't manage on my own. I must have twisted my ankle,' she invented rapidly, wickedly enjoying getting her own way. 'I can't put much weight on it. That's what held me up.'

Let him wriggle out of that! Hobbling at his side, she would slow him down considerably. Hopefully, they'd meet Janet on her way back, having kissed her lover a fond farewell and pulled herself together.

Although it was too dark for them to see each other, she could sense his eyes on her, feel his impatience even before he verbalised it.

'I'll take you back.' He sounded as if he would rather lie down in front of a runaway steamroller. He took the torch from her, clicking it back on, the bright beam illuminating the narrow track.

'Forgotten Janet?' she reminded him. It would be far better, for his fiancée's sake, if he didn't go near the Manor tonight, but she had to make a token protest.

'She wasn't expecting me to meet her,' he muttered tersely. 'She has a torch and knows her way blindfold. Can you walk at all, or do I have to carry you?'

The thought of him carrying her, of being held in those strong arms, tight against that superbly fit body, horrified her. And not because such physical closeness would stimulate all the sensual need she'd discovered in herself. No, of course not! But because—because… Oh, she was too confused to think!

'I can manage!' she said crossly.

'You said you couldn't.'

'To hobble!' she snapped right back, demonstrating that when it came to curtness she could be as expert as he.

'Then you'd better lean on me.' He sounded as if help was the last thing he wanted to give her, a one-way ticket to some remote spot in the Amazon Basin being more to his liking.

She took his arm, her throat tightening up as the heat from his body scorched her, her self-respect at its lowest ebb yet as she felt his body tense with distaste at having to endure her touch.

Yet he had been happy to touch her earlier. To kiss her, even, and to flatter her, giving her new confidence in herself. And now he was giving out all the opposite signals. It could only mean that he believed she had read far more into the situation than he'd meant.

So he'd deliberately gone all distant and disagreeable, as good as telling her to get out of his sight with the least possible delay because he was secretly afraid she might go all moony over him, trail around after him with her tongue hanging out like a twelve-year-old schoolgirl drooling over a pop star! Just because he had kissed her!

It demonstrated what an over-inflated ego he had. It insulted her. He was a vain, ruthless, cold-blooded bastard, and she couldn't imagine how she could ever have felt physically attracted to him, drawn to him...

And yet walking with him, leaning against his arm, she wasn't having to pretend to hobble. His very closeness, the warmth of his body, the faint, spicy male scent of him, was sending her heartbeats haywire, making her dizzy, her legs almost too weak to hold her at all...

She didn't want to feel like this. It made her lose her self-respect, made her hate him even more for having this power over her. She wished she'd taken the torch when he'd offered, let him go ahead and discover Janet's secret guilt. Let them sort it out between them. She hadn't wanted to get involved, hadn't meant to, wished she hadn't...

Her swamping confusion and misery made her lose her footing altogether, and she cried out with shock at the electrifying sensation as his arm immediately snaked around her waist, supporting her as her small weight fell against his body.

'To hell with this!' he swore grimly, mistaking her cry of shock for one of pain and sweeping her up in his arms and striding through the last of the trees as if the hounds of hell were baying at his heels.

It was torment. Her ragged emotions tugged this way and that.

When they reached the house she mustered all her

mental strength and told him frostily, 'Put me down now. I can manage from here.' If necessary she would tell him her damaged ankle had made a miraculous recovery and demonstrate it by pounding up the stairs, packing her bags and leaving the two of them to organise their own wedding!

He ignored her, his features grimly set as he carried her over the hall and up the staircase. And the total contempt he showed her by not even deigning to acknowledge her words, by treating her as if she were not even human, just a damn nuisance, a burden he wanted to rid himself of sooner than immediately, brought tears gushing unstoppably to her eyes.

The tears made her hate herself as much as she hated him! They demeaned her utterly. She should be adult enough, woman enough, strong enough to be completely unaffected by anything he said or did. She tried to blink them away but they trickled humiliatingly down her cheeks.

He shouldered open her bedroom door, then pushed it closed with his foot.

The windows were open, the breeze pushing against the curtains bringing with it the scent of honeysuckle, and the moon had risen now, dispelling the darkness, filling the beautiful room with a silvery shimmering light.

Enough light for him to see his way to the bed, to dump her on the pristine white coverlet. Reaching past her, he snapped on the bedside light, the radiance softly flooding through the gold silk shade.

There was enough light and radiance now for her to see that strong-boned face, the curiously hard and shuttered eyes. Free from his despised burden, he folded his arms across his chest, his eyes fixed firmly on her feet.

'I suppose you're here until the ankle mends? Unless I get Tossie to drive you home tomorrow. I could follow in your car and come back with her.'

She ignored the pain of that. She shouldn't care. She wouldn't let herself care. Her chin went up.

'My, what lengths to get rid of me! But don't worry, I shall be perfectly capable of driving myself, so you won't have to put yourself to that much trouble.'

She had been going to add that she was not prepared to handle his commission any more, but couldn't think of a reason for quitting that would sound in the least bit professional. And that mattered to her—especially now he'd dented her self-esteem so effectively.

'I'll leave the moment I've seen the designer. My assistant will handle everything else, and leave me free to concentrate on my other clients,' she compromised, and endured the dark stab of his eyes before they fastened back on her feet.

'As you like.' He sounded indifferent. 'As for driving, it wouldn't be safe if you've sprained an ankle. It's obviously hurting, or you wouldn't have been crying. I'm not particularly up on medical practice, but common sense tells me it should be strapped until you can get home and have your doctor take a look at it.'

So he had noticed her damp cheeks, but, thankfully, he had got the source of her misery all wrong.

Before she had cottoned on to his intention, he had hunkered down in front of her and was regarding both her ankles with deep suspicion.

'Which one hurts?' he demanded, his voice low and silky but a threat all the same. 'Neither is swollen.'

Strong, inescapable hands removed both shoes, and when she tried to push her feet under the bed, out of his reach, he captured them easily, his invading fingers gentle now as they probed both slender ankles, sliding up to her shapely calves and slowly down again, flexing her toes, and back again to circle her ankles.

Alice closed her eyes, gritting her teeth. This was sheer torture! There wasn't any pain, of course there wasn't, simply unendurable sexual torture! His touch had the impact of an earthquake, and the tension of hiding it from him was building up inside her like an explosion waiting to happen.

It was almost a relief when he said softly, 'Liar! There is nothing remotely wrong with either of your ankles.'

Her eyes fluttered open as he stood up, and she swallowed a whimper—half in relief because he'd stopped touching her, and half in anguish because she'd never seen him looking like this before. As if he was bone-weary, all the life gone out of his eyes, his features harsh, austere. He looked unreachable, as if he was being driven by private devils, carrying a burden no one else could share.

And the implications of what he'd just said were crystal-clear. He knew she hadn't hurt herself, knew she'd been perfectly capable of getting back under her own steam when he'd given her the torch. Knew she'd lied. He didn't know the reason for it, but he obviously thought he did.

'Why lie?' he demanded grittily. 'You could have got back on your own—and don't bother denying it. For God's sake, Alice, get off my case, will you?'

If there was a plea in his voice she ignored it. Even if he thought she was chasing him, what was there to worry about? She'd already said she'd be gone in the morning. What more did he want? He was overreacting—far too colourfully. Courtroom drama rubbing off, she supposed.

She glared at him mutinously, refusing to answer his question. She couldn't anyway. She had painted herself into a corner. She couldn't deny that she'd lied. He knew she hadn't hurt her wretched ankle. But she couldn't drop Janet in it—not when she'd begged Alice to say nothing.

Not able to defend herself, she attacked. Blisteringly.

'Listen to me! I may not be so all-fired bright in the upper storey as you but I'm not stupid!' She jerked to her feet, her hands on her hips, her glasses slipping down her nose. 'You've been treating me like dirt all evening, and don't think I don't know why! You think I got all dressed up to attract you into a bit of pre-marital indiscretion. Well, I've got news for you. I didn't.

'So you kissed me—well, that was no big deal!' Her eyes speared him, adrenalin running high and wild. 'Because I can tell you here and now it didn't turn me on. As far as excitement went, it rated slightly lower than when my cousin kissed me at my birthday party. I was five and he was three!'

'Liar!' The tone of his voice was a dark threat.

Raw, menacing danger glittered in his eyes, stopping the tide of her hectic words—lying words.

She had wounded his massive ego, his masculine pride. He wanted revenge and would take it, and all she could feel was the sting of anticipation, the excitement of having him as an open adversary, having him as her clear-cut enemy because she couldn't have him as anything else.

'You're having trouble with that?' she challenged, flipping her tumbled hair back from her face. 'Hurts, does it? Knowing some females exist who don't take one look at you and fall in adoring, lustful heaps at your feet?'

She suffered the consequences of her sharp little tongue as he growled something dark and emotional at the back of his throat and gathered her ruthlessly into his arms, his mouth a hungry possession as he took her lips and showed her the true, wild meaning of passion...

CHAPTER EIGHT

HE KISSED her with fiery, passionate hunger, branding her, sweeping her away on a storm of rioting emotions. Wild physical desire, savage anger. That Gideon could do this to her, that he could make her respond to his sexual potency, scorched Alice with voracious anger.

Fiercely, she kissed him back—a wild punishment for what he was: an unholy fallen angel. A tormenting castigation for what he'd made of her: a wanton, a mindless creature of savage passion.

And when he broke the kiss the punishment was far from over, rebounding on them both. Her skin was hot, breasts swelling, every muscle tight with raw tension. And as he caught her head into the hollow of his shoulder his breathing was as harsh as hers.

Far from ending, it was just beginning. A whimper of anguish caught in her throat, a plea for release from his wicked magic. But it was only beginning—she knew that, her body knew that, opening, flowering, no denial offered, no defences.

Captor and captivated, both. Both caught now in the relentless, urgent tide of need, both drowning in desire as he stroked the tumbled hair back from her face and pressed fervent kisses down the length of her throat.

Drowning and lost as her small hands slid lovingly down his body, exploring the magnificent perfection

118

of him, she saw his eyes close, felt his hard body tremble. Tiny shudders gripped his firm flesh with fevered torment, and when his mouth took hers again it was insanity, a wild, sweet pain that surged liquidly through her limbs, making her melt into the heated hardness of him.

And behind closed, drugged eyes sprang the painted hallucination of two others. Two others lost in the sweet violence of passion.

Janet and Will, as she'd seen them, the aura of just such an emotional turbulence surrounding them, making the air throb, sing to a sweet, sad wildness.

'Don't! For God's sake, don't!' She pushed at his body with frenzied hands, her eyes feverish, burning and dark in the sudden pallor of her face. 'I'm here to organise a wedding, for pity's sake! Yours and Janet's!' she ground out into his shocked silence.

He looked stunned, momentarily pole-axed, like a man in the grip of a trauma. Then he dragged in a harsh breath, his voice ragged as he told her, 'Alice. We must talk.'

'No,' she countered fiercely, backing away. Afraid. Of him. Of herself. Of what she was capable of feeling. Of the need, the terrible, driving need. Just for this man, who was not hers to crave.

'We have to.' Determined, he moved closer, his face still, austere. Beneath the thick fringe of dark lashes was the glitter of intense emotion. She could see the black line that rimmed the breathtaking blue, the tiny shards of silver that made them gleam like rain-washed blue diamonds, and could have died of longing. And despair. Then anger came to her rescue.

'Just get out. Leave me alone.' Her voice was bitter. 'I don't want to see you or speak to you. Haven't you done enough damage?' Hysteria was starting now, thinning her voice, shaking it, the sensation of breaking up beginning deep inside her. 'Get out,' she threatened, right on the edge now. 'Or I'll scream the house down!'

She saw his eyes narrow, his mouth harden. He was very pale.

'Tomorrow,' he said harshly, and the single word hit her like a threat. She froze to rigid stillness, barely breathing until he'd walked out of the room and closed the door quietly behind him.

She leapt to it like a whirlwind, locked it, then slowly, her back to the polished wood, slid down it, encircling her head with her arms as it sank heavily to her raised knees. Hating herself. Hating him.

She was cold, her bones aching, every muscle stiff when she crawled into bed at dawn. Gradually, at long last, she tumbled into a heavy, unrefreshing sleep and was woken by someone trying to open her door.

Gideon?

Her heart thudded heavily. He would give her no peace. He had taken her into his arms, taken his revenge, and had threatened to talk to her. And they would be hateful words, extracting her promise to say nothing about what had happened.

Feeling sick and demeaned, she ignored him, thankful for the instinct that had made her lock the door.

And then he knocked. A tentative tap or two at first, and then more insistently. She bit back the need to call out to him, tell him to get lost. She wouldn't give him the satisfaction of any communication.

But the voice that called her name wasn't his.

Janet. Insistent.

Alice fumbled on the night-table for her glasses and shoved them on, askew, blinking blearily at her watch. Had she slept in late? Had Nico arrived?

But the slender fingers showed it was barely six-thirty. Brows pleating, she rolled off the bed and draped the coverlet around her. She had dragged off her dress and fallen into bed in her bra and briefs, and she needed to cover the body that had become hateful to her. How could she not be ashamed of something that had so flagrantly betrayed her?

'Did I wake you?' Janet asked as the door opened a crack. Her face was pale, her eyes red-rimmed, her shoulders bowed as if she carried the sorrows of the world on her narrow back. 'I was sure you'd be awake already. Those sirens—'

'Sirens?' Alice parroted, opening the door fully and stepping aside, feeling too bleary-eyed and heavy to think. Janet didn't look as if she'd slept much either.

'Ten minutes or so ago. One of the emergency services. I was sure the whole household must be awake. Must have been a traffic accident down in the lanes.' She shuddered, wrapping her arms around her thin body, clad, as seemed usual, in scuffed jeans and an old T-shirt. 'Horrible! I do hope no one I know was involved. Or is that being selfish?'

She was walking round the room stiffly, her arms still clamped around her body. Then she shook her head impatiently. 'I didn't come here to talk about that. It's got nothing to do with it—only that I thought you must be already awake. Listen, about last night…'

Alice went weak with horror and sank down on the bed, clutching the coverlet more tightly around her. Had Gideon confessed? Told his bride-to-be what had happened here, in this very room? Explained that the mouthy little bitch had told him that he was less exciting than the three-year-old who had kissed her at her fifth birthday party? Made him so angry that he'd been forced to teach her otherwise? Getting his side of the story in before she opened her mouth and spat out the poison?

She sagged with shamed relief when Janet said shakily, 'Last night. What you saw. Me and—'

'It isn't any of my business, really it isn't!' Alice broke in quickly, relief that it wasn't her sins under discussion making her babble.

'It is your business.' Janet managed to give her a direct look for the first time. She even produced a wan smile. 'I don't want you thinking that all your work will have been for nothing. The wedding will go ahead, as planned. My mother wants it, Gideon wants it, and up until recently—when Will and I first met—I wanted it.'

And despite her own misery, her preoccupation with self-loathing, Alice discovered she had enough emotional capability left to find sympathy.

'If you're in love with someone else—and from what you've just said I take it you are—then you can't marry Gideon because your mother wants you to.'

'It's not that simple.' Janet stood at a window, looking out. 'I only wish it were. And, yes, I am in love with Will. It hit us both. Hard. But by the time he came into my life I'd already promised to marry Gideon. I'd been really content with that, you see. I've known him all my life and I've always loved him. But like a brother. I thought that would be enough. Affection, respect. And it would have been, if I hadn't met Will and discovered what real love was.

'He'll leave, of course,' she said bleakly. 'He can't stay on when I'm married to Gideon. Neither of us could bear that. So he'll go and we'll never see each other again. We spent last night saying goodbye to each other.' She flushed faintly, catching her breath before she went on. 'I think we owed each other that much.' The look she gave Alice was defiant. 'I'll be completely faithful to Gideon when we're married!'

But would he be faithful to her? With all that potent sexuality, a little black book stuffed with telephone numbers, a wife he didn't love, who didn't love him? Alice doubted it.

She pushed that thought out of her mind. Janet needed her help. By the sound of it she needed all the help she could get if she wasn't to end up making a complete mess of her life.

'You've got to be off your trolley!' she said firmly, her brows drawing together. 'Why not tell Gideon the truth? Tell him you've fallen in love with someone else and can't go through with the marriage. Engagements aren't sacrosanct, for pity's sake—unlike wedding vows, which darn well should be! He wouldn't want a wife who was secretly yearning for someone else!'

'He would never know. I'd make sure of that.' Janet shrugged helplessly. 'Basically, he wants a wife who won't do a runner, like his mother. She was a famous beauty, by all accounts. Vain and skittish. When married life became a bore she ran out, never giving a thought to the child she left behind, wondering where his mummy had gone, when she'd be coming back.

'But she didn't come back, and it left its mark on him. A mark his father made sure didn't fade. He was a bitter man, for all he divorced his wife and married Rose. Good, plain, sensible Rose. Now she was a real mother to Gideon. They've always been very close and I guess he'd have become as bitter as his father if it hadn't been for her. As it is, he's just a bit cynical about beautiful women. He enjoys them, just as any man would, but he doesn't trust them.'

She pulled her mouth in wryly. 'That's why, when he decided to settle down, build a family, he proposed to me. I'm suitable. Sensible—well, I was until I took one look at Will and went overboard. Ordinary, safe, loyal.

'Do you know—' she turned and gave Alice a bleak smile '—he once said that the temporary insanity people call falling in love is no sound basis for what should be a lifetime of living together because that sort of hormonal imbalance never lasts?

'But naturally he wants children some day, and I guess he sees me as coming from the same mould as Rose. He is fond of me, he likes me, and he would never do anything to harm me. And, believe me, there are other considerations which make our marriage essential—make it impossible for me to back out of the arrangement.'

'Like property?' Alice blurted. She couldn't stop

the words. Hadn't she suspected something like this all along? Could the man who had admitted he had no time for the emotion of falling in love, calling it a temporary insanity, be so driven by the need to acquire the valuable Manor property, the rich lands that so conveniently abutted his own, that he would stoop to somehow blackmailing poor Janet into agreeing to be his wife?

And was that—the dark, ruthless streak in the man—the very thing that had drawn her, made her want him until her flesh had burned and quivered on her bones? Was that where his magic lay for her? Oh, heaven save her from herself!

Janet, after a long moment of silence, answered her question, whispering almost inaudibly, 'You're right. It all comes down to property. I'm sorry, but I can't talk about that aspect of it. But I'm glad you listened. It helped, I think.'

She left the room quietly, walking like an old woman, leaving Alice with her horrible suspicions verified. Vilifying herself.

How could she have been so fatally attracted to such a man? A blackmailing devil with not a principle worth mentioning. Why else should Janet, who was deeply in love with Will Gaunt, have agreed to marry Gideon Rymer if he didn't have a hold over her?

'Come in, Nico. We'll find Janet, have a coffee and make a start.'

Alice's smile was fixed firmly in place. She had been waiting on the drive for the last five minutes, her hair neatly back in its braid, shivering a little in her grey business suit because today was chilly, overcast. Summer seemed to have gone and it was almost like winter again, to match the winter in her heart.

Thankfully, Nico had arrived punctually at ten, and when this was over she could get in her car and drive away and nothing would stop her.

'Hiya!' He had a very white smile and was, she supposed, what was popularly known as a dish—long dark hair in a ponytail, just the fashionable amount of designer stubble, and if he hadn't designed his suit himself then Armani had.

He retrieved his portfolio and sketch-block from the passenger seat of his Porsche and Alice looked furtively over her shoulder. No sign of Gideon. She never wanted to have to face him again.

They walked together into the house and Alice put him in the sitting room then went to rout Janet out from wherever she was hiding.

Alice wouldn't blame her at all if she'd done a runner, taken off with Will Gaunt, disregarding blackmail and everything else Gideon could throw at them. But more probably she was psyching herself up to the point where she could actually bear to pretend an interest in what she would wear on her wedding day.

Alice hadn't seen her since she'd left her room at seven that morning. She hadn't seen anyone, skipping breakfast because she couldn't face it—or Gideon—doing her packing, having a bath, washing and braiding her hair.

She had been hiding from a problem for the very first time in her life. But she didn't regret taking the coward's way out. She felt bad enough about what had happened last night without him swearing her to secrecy, piling on the agony. Because why else should he have insisted on their need to talk?

Janet and Gwen were walking down the stairs together so at least she didn't have to go on a room-to-room hunt, running the risk of encountering Gideon. Janet looked pale but composed, hiding her haunted eyes behind her lovely smile.

Gwen said, 'I'm going to sit in on the session. If I like the young man's work I'm going to ask him to design something for me. I can afford it now, and Ralph would have wanted me to look my best for our daughter's wedding.'

Then her eyes lost that anxious look as she added, 'Jan and I will be collecting Rose from the airport this afternoon. She phoned last night to say she'd cut her holiday short. I'll be glad to have her home; she always knows what to do...'

Trying to make the right responses, Alice pushed open the sitting-room door, made the introductions and sat in a corner. Her own distasteful work was finished now that she had herded the unfortunate Janet to where she understandably didn't want to be, to consult with the designer she hadn't wanted to see over a dress she didn't want to have to wear.

She had to admire the girl's stoicism, but she couldn't condone the way she was giving in to blackmail, throwing away her chance of real happiness. What kind of hold could Gideon possibly have over her? Was it something so dreadful she couldn't contemplate toughing it out, even for the sake of the man she loved? It had to be.

Alice sighed, gazing restlessly around her, longing to be gone. The French windows were firmly closed this morning, and a coal-effect electric fire had been plugged in, standing in place of the huge floral arrangement that had been in the hearth yesterday.

There would be a comforting living fire in that hearth in the winter time, she guessed. She could just see Janet and Gideon sitting around it in the years to come, their children with them, and her heart squeezed so painfully she gasped aloud.

Thankfully, no one had heard. Nico was holding forth, making slashing movements with his charcoal on a sheet of paper, and Alice wondered if she could slip away now, leave them to it. There was nothing more for her to do.

Mentally finding excuses—an afternoon appointment would do—she gathered her handbag, thought longingly of the packed suitcase waiting in her room and of her little car snugly parked in the stable block, got to her feet—and sat straight down again as Gideon walked in.

He was wearing soft, worn old denims that rode low on his hips and moulded themselves to his endless legs like a second skin. An ancient sweatshirt, the colour of teak, and a pair of dusty boots completed his outfit, and for the first time since she'd known him he looked harried.

She wanted to look away but couldn't. He mesmerised her. All she could think of was the way she had felt when he'd held her in his arms, close, outrageously close to that achingly fantastic body. She remembered the wild, punishing passion as they'd kissed, the memory branded on her brain, her responses to him programmed into her for all time.

She shuddered and watched his dark brows bunch

as he took in the busy group at the other end of the room then strode directly towards her. There was a smudge of dust along one cheekbone, but that only heightened the perfection of him. And his eyes were dark. Intent. Looking only at her now, pinning her to her seat.

Last night he had threatened her with the need to talk. Here? Now? She almost panicked. If he was intent on warning her against saying anything about what had happened last night, upsetting Janet, she would feel indescribably cheap. She really couldn't cope with that. Yet why else should he be making a beeline for her?

'Alice—' His rough velvet voice was pitched low, but she could hear the strain. He really did think she was the type to kiss and tell.

Her eyes slid angrily away from his, and her heart was beating so thunderously she could barely hear his rawly whispered words.

'I would have found you sooner than this—' his broad shoulders lifted impatiently '—but Will phoned at dawn. There was a barn fire at the home farm. I had to get over there fast. It's out now; the fire service were quick off the mark. I have to get back there again, though.

'I went to your room five minutes ago and your bags are packed. Stay.' His voice was compelling. She stared at her shoes. 'I'll be about an hour. We have to talk—you know we do. Wait for me. You'll do that?'

'Yes,' she lied, willing him to go away, saying what he wanted to hear to get rid of him. She had no intention of waiting to hear him tell her to keep quiet about last night. He could stew. If he thought she was that type of woman then he deserved sleepless nights.

Her eyes smouldering, she watched him walk over to Janet, bend over, speak to her. With an apology, the other girl left the room with the man she was going to marry even though she didn't want to. Alice composed herself to wait.

The louse didn't love his future bride; he coveted her property. But he wouldn't want her to learn that he'd come within a whisker of making love to their wedding organiser. That might make her jealous, turn her into a suspicious, nagging wife.

After ten minutes, and with no sign of Janet returning, Alice decided she'd had enough. She went over to where Nico was deep in conversation with Gwen, covering a foolscap sheet of paper with bold, flowing lines.

'I'll be on my way,' she said, interrupting the consultation gently. 'An appointment to keep—you know how it is. Tell Janet I'll keep an eye on the way everything's shaping up from the office, but if she runs into any problems she can contact me straight away.'

Not that there would be any. Because she had no option. Janet would be married in her designer gown and Gideon would keep her in the lap of luxury and give her beautiful children. And he'd make good and sure his infidelities were never discovered—witness his single-minded insistence on ensuring that Alice kept her mouth tightly buttoned.

In time Janet would forget Will, or he'd become little more than a misty memory, and if she thought of him at all it would be like coming across a faded flower, pressed between the pages of a book, and wondering why you'd put it there in the first place. And she would eventually become content. Not happy, of course. But content, which was more than a lot of people managed.

Realising that her hands were balling into fists, Alice straightened them out as Dona came in with a coffee-tray. That gave her the chance to say her good-byes and thank-yous and slip away.

She couldn't wait to get away from Rymer Court and everyone in it. The whole experience had become a nightmare and she couldn't wait to fight her way out of it and get on with her sane and satisfactory life again.

CHAPTER NINE

ALICE drifted into sleep and almost immediately came fuzzily awake yet again. She turned on the narrow bed and groaned. The effort of pulling air into her burning lungs used up all her energy.

Her skin heavily dewed with sweat, she kicked feebly at the sheet and reached for the stool that served as a bedside table, knocking the box of tissues to the floor and failing to find her glasses.

They were probably on the floor too, or she'd put them down someplace else. She couldn't remember. But without them she couldn't read the time on her watch.

Flopping back on the lumpy mattress, she gave up. Time didn't matter. It could be as much as forty-eight hours before the viral symptoms were over. Yesterday—it had been yesterday, hadn't it?—had been her first full day back at the office, and by midday she'd been shivering, all her bones aching, her head about to split open, so she would have at least another twenty-four hours of misery to get through...

At least the nausea had passed, and the worst of the stomach cramps, and if she could do something about her raging thirst she might be able to get some proper sleep. But getting herself out of bed, crossing the room to the sink to get a glass of water was beyond her...

And it was so hot, stifling in the airless, shabby

room she called home. Summer had returned with all the stops pulled out…

The banging broke through her fretful sleep. At first she thought the hammers inside her head had started up again, but then everything went silent and all she could hear was the rasping of her own breath.

And then the sound of a key turning in the lock.

Probably her landlord—no one else had a key. She frowned, wondering if the rent was overdue. No, surely it couldn't be. She was always meticulous about paying her bills. Or perhaps the building was on fire, she thought listlessly, too tired to care. Whatever, at least she could ask him to bring her some water.

Ineffectual hands tugged weakly at the hem of the old T-shirt she wore to bed and tried to locate the sheet her feverish wallowings had thrown somewhere. Tolly Brent's eyes might be old and rheumy, but he wasn't blind and she wasn't so far gone in fever that she'd lost all sense of modesty.

'You!' she croaked as Gideon's set features loomed over her. She passed a shaky hand over her eyes to wipe the fever-induced hallucination away. He had stalked through the snatches of her restless dreams ever since she'd been taken ill, his face the only constant in the nightmarish muddles thrown up by her subconscious, haunting her.

Frantically now, she tugged at her T-shirt. It had got all rucked up around her waist. And she knew he was real, not just a tormenting fantasy, when one strong hand eased her back against the pillow and the other brushed aside her damp and tumbled hair then pressed gently against her burning forehead.

His fingers were dry and cool, taking away her headache for a blessed moment or two, making her whimper with the first relief she'd had in what felt like days, and then he straightened, turning away.

Alice whimpered again. She didn't mean to but she couldn't help it. He was leaving. Disgusted with her, with the state she was in? Annoyed with her? Yes, that had to be it. And she would remember exactly why if she tried hard enough, but she couldn't summon the mental energy.

She could hear him moving around now, though, opening cupboards, the door of the tiny fridge which was at the end of the room laughably described by Tolly as the 'kitchenette'. And then she heard him talking, and he had to be using her phone because no one responded, not that she could hear. So he hadn't left.

Unaccountably soothed, she sagged back against the pillow and closed her gritty eyes…

She woke to find herself in his arms. Her heart gave a feeble jerk and she tried to say his name and ask him to please keep holding her because it felt wonderful, made her feel safe, but her throat was so dry she could only manage a croak.

'It's all right, Alice,' he said soothingly. 'I'm looking after you now.'

Had anyone ever told him what a beautiful voice he had? she wondered vaguely, relaxing bonelessly against him. Deep and dark, but warm too. Comforting, reassuring. And he smelt so fresh: clean and cool with a hint of lemon, a hint of spice. And he—

And he was tugging at the hem of her battered

T-shirt, dragging it up over her head. Some atavistic instinct made her try to fight him off, but he made soothing shushing noises and she gave up.

As he pulled the damp garment away she allowed her head to flop forward against his shoulder, her hot face buried in the cool, crisp cotton of his shirt.

'Good girl.' His arms were so strong, his voice so soft, encouraging her. 'I'm going to try to make you more comfortable, and there's a doctor on his way. Not your GP, but a friend of mine from the private sector.'

Harley Street, Alice thought, the cool water he was gently sponging her with clearing her head a little. So that was who she'd heard him phoning.

She would have told him she didn't need a doctor, thanks all the same, that everyone knew that viruses went away in their own good time. But a sudden attack of the shivers made her teeth chatter. She stopped thinking of anything except how wonderful it was to be held like this, in his arms, warmly, gently, until the shivering stopped.

He eased her into a fresh T-shirt, somehow fitted the rumpled bed with clean, cool linen and propped her up against the plumped-up pillow, holding a glass for her while she thirstily emptied it of water.

And then he left her, and when he came back there was someone else with him. A neat, slim man, in an expensive pearl-grey suit, who took her pulse and put his stethoscope all over her front and back and told her to breathe in and out until she felt too ill to be bothered and told him to go away.

'Drink this,' Gideon said.

It could have been hours later, or only minutes; she

didn't know. He supported her while she obediently drank the draught and when she shuddered at the taste and screwed up her face in disgust he grinned at her.

'Don't be such a baby! It's to bring your temperature down and help with the aches and pains. Otherwise, so Temple told me, you'll be back to normal in a couple of days. Plenty to drink, plenty of sleep. Now, I'll be out for half an hour. OK?'

He eased her back against the pillow, brushed her hair away from her forehead and tucked the sheet up under her chin.

'There's nothing in your fridge but half a carton of stale milk and nothing in the cupboards apart from a few teabags and a tin of beans.' He shot her a suddenly grim look. 'Are you so busy organising other people's lives that you have no time to do anything about your own?'

She opened her mouth to tell him that she organised other people's weddings, not their lives, and that reminded her—shouldn't he be getting back to poor, sad Janet? But she took one look at his face and thought better of it.

She wondered, with the first sense of lucidity she'd known for many long hours, exactly what he was doing here, why he had come. But she didn't ask that either, because she didn't like the hint of ferocity in his glittering eyes, and his mouth looked positively dangerous.

She clamped her own lips together and closed her eyes on a sudden spurt of tears, waiting until she heard the door close behind him before she cried herself silly and fell asleep.

*   *   *

'You look better.'

Awakening to find him sitting on the edge of the bed, Alice did a rapid internal inventory and discovered she did feel better than she had when he'd first found her. Though whether it was down to his still being here, watching her with approval instead of that earlier grim impatience, or due to the noxious draught she'd swallowed, she didn't know.

A bit of both, she supposed, accepting the glass of deliciously chilled orange juice he gave her and sipping thirstily.

He had opened the window and the evening air was comparatively fresh—well, for a London back in the grip of an early heatwave it was. And there were around a dozen gorgeous white lilies in the chunky stoneware pot Amaryllis had received as a wedding gift and handed on because she hated it.

'Flowers!' she said, delighted, wondering why he'd bothered.

He told her, subduing her utterly, 'You need something to brighten this depressing place. Life isn't worth living if there's no beauty in it.'

He took the empty glass from her, his dark brows pulled down. She remembered Tossie once saying that he liked to be surrounded by beautiful things—and that obviously included women, of course. She sighed deeply because she knew she looked about as appealing as her unlovely room right now.

'Why do you do it?' he asked her edgily. 'This place is a dump, yet your business is doing well—don't you think you deserve any better? Is that it? Do you think so little of yourself?'

Without giving her the opportunity to get a word

in edgewise in self-defence, he grimly ploughed straight on, 'Is it yet another hang-up from when you were a kid, growing up with three beautiful sisters who made you feel plain and second-rate? If so, you need re-educating. Fast.' He stood up abruptly, his face set, and took the glass over to the sink.

Weak tears stung the back of her eyes. She remembered, far too vividly, the way he had set about teaching her to believe she was kissable and felt herself quiver. She wanted nothing to do with his brand of tuition! And why was he so angry, anyway? Why should he give a damn where she lived, or how? And why should his opinion bother her?

There was no answer to that, or none she dared contemplate. So she hoisted herself up on one elbow and shot at him, 'If you don't like my home you know what you can do! I didn't ask you to come, and I can't imagine why you did. How did you get hold of the key anyway?' she tacked on accusingly, pushing her tangled hair out of her hands with one savage swipe.

She saw the rigid line of his shoulders gradually relax, watched him turn slowly on the balls of his feet, his hands thrust deep in the pockets of the lightweight dark trousers he wore. He was smiling, not angry, not now, and that was like the sun coming out on a dark winter's day. And in that one small moment, that one awesome moment, Alice knew she had done the unthinkable, the impossible, the unbearable.

She had fallen in love. She loved Gideon Rymer with the whole of her passionate heart.

And no use denying it, she mourned, watching him as he took two paces to the rickety table that took up most of the centre of the narrow room. He leaned against it, watching her.

It wasn't because he was the most sexually potent, charismatic man she'd ever encountered. And his moral fibre, or decided lack of it where his marriage plans were concerned, didn't come into it. It was simply because it seemed fated. Inevitable. She was drawn to the man, body and soul. Everything she was belonged to him and he belonged to someone else.

The knowledge was appalling.

'I came up to town because there's unfinished business between us.' He was answering her questions and she could barely focus on what he was saying. She looked at him despairingly then quickly lowered her eyes. He mustn't guess what she was feeling. Never. Ever!

'I wasn't in the best of moods,' he said to her downcast head. 'You'd promised to stay on at Rymer. All I asked was that you should wait for an hour. One miserable hour.'

The memory of what had happened that last night she'd spent under his roof bound her to him with an intimacy that was shocking. They'd come so near to making love, hurled towards breaking point on a tide of wild passion.

Thank heaven she'd come to her senses, reminded him of where his loyalties lay!

Her stomach curled and she sucked her bottom lip between her teeth. What could she say? That she'd fled like a coward because she hadn't wanted to hear him warn her against saying anything to Janet, because hearing him actually speak the words would have made that wild interlude in his arms seem sordid and cheap? She had been falling in love with him since she'd first seen him; she knew that now.

She shook her head in mute misery, beyond making excuses, and thankfully he seemed to expect no explanation from her, not at this point.

He spoke again, his tone lighter. 'When I got to your office your assistant told me you were home, nursing a virus. And she gave me your address when I told her, not untruthfully, that there was something vitally important I had to discuss with you. If she took that to mean changes to the wedding arrangements, fair enough.'

At his offhand mention of those she hardened her heart. She had to. It was either that or burst into over-emotional tears at the cruel reminder of what a duplicitous louse he really was, despite his extravagantly gorgeous looks and charming, caring manner.

She glared at him and he tilted an eyebrow.

'Don't read her the riot act. She was cagey at first, insisting she had the expertise to deal with any problem. But I can be very persuasive.'

And didn't she know it!

'Persuasion got you the key to let yourself in, I suppose?' she muttered crossly, and earned herself a cool smile.

'That and telling the old man who I was. At the mention of anything remotely connected with the law your landlord became remarkably servile.' He levered himself away from the table and shot a look at his watch. 'It's almost time for your next dose of medication, but food first. Could you manage scrambled eggs?'

She shook her head. The very thought of eating

made her feel queasy, and she felt light-headed again, weak. Trying to hold her own with him, trying to come to terms with the terrible discovery of loving him had taken far more out of her than she would have thought possible.

'Just go,' she said shakily. 'Thanks for all you've done. But just go. I don't want you here.' She sank feebly back against the pillow and knew she was lying. She *did* want him here, now and always, with her, a part of her, loving her as she loved him. And that was impossible. 'Won't Janet be wondering where you are?'

And that was said less to remind him that he had other obligations and more to remind herself, to harden herself against him. But all it managed to do was to produce a savage pain in her heart. She closed her eyes to hide the sudden tears.

'I'm going nowhere while you're in this state,' he informed her sharply, totally disregarding her painful mention of his soon-to-be wife. 'I'll go when you're fit to look after yourself, and then only after we've had that talk you owe me.'

Far too feeble to argue, insist, she turned her face to the wall and wondered why he was hanging around—by his own admission prepared to stay as long as it took, until she was in a fit state to listen to what he had to say.

She heard him moving around and roused herself when he brought her medication, drinking the glass of juice he held for her before turning her face to the wall again and slipping in and out of restless sleep.

She needed oblivion, craved it, but she couldn't keep him from wandering in and out of her mind.

He must be desperate for her promise to hold her tongue about what had happened that night... He had to be determined to marry poor Janet for financial gain... Couldn't afford to give her the handle she needed to call it off, his promiscuity negating whatever hold he had over her... And whatever that hold was it was strong enough to prevent her from going to the man she really loved... What had Janet said? 'There are other considerations which make our marriage essential...'

Property...

When she finally struggled up out of patchy sleep the room was in darkness apart from the dim glow from a table-lamp on the other side of the room. It illuminated the fabled 'kitchenette', the rusty fridge, the solitary gas ring and chipped enamel sink.

Gideon was sprawled in the saggy armchair, apparently asleep. Though how anyone could sleep on that, with all those broken springs and lumpy cushions, was beyond her.

She had often thought of replacing most of the stuff in the furnished bedsit, but when it had come to the crunch she had always decided against it. The money would be far better placed in her business, and nobody ever came here except herself.

Even so, she regretted the armchair. The poor love would wake up aching in every joint.

But he wasn't a 'poor love', she reminded herself tartly. He was a rich bastard who would stoop to blackmail, and ruin poor Janet's life into the bargain, to make himself even richer.

And she needed to go to the bathroom.

Gingerly, she slid her legs out of bed, careful not

to wake him. In the dim light he looked mouth-wateringly gorgeous. Just looking at him made her heart pound, her breath catch in her throat. So she looked quickly away and bent to fish her dressing gown out from under the bed—and fell in a heap, sending the stool clattering onto its side, as dizziness came at her in great whirling black clouds.

Which woke the sleeping tiger.

He was out of the chair and with her in one spring-loaded bound, hauling her to her feet, his fingers biting into her arms.

'What the hell do you think you're doing?'

Alice blinked, trying to get his face into focus. He was in an almighty rage, shouting at her, she thought with mild detachment, wondering why—until he told her.

'If you want something, you call out. Understand?'

He looked mad enough to shake her until her teeth rattled, she decided, her head beginning to feel as if it belonged to her again. At least the room wasn't spinning round in ever decreasing circles.

'I need to go to the bathroom,' she managed loftily. 'I don't think even you can do that for me.'

'Fine.' She thought she saw his mouth quirk but couldn't be sure. And, although she felt very much better, when his hands slid away from her she swayed, her legs threatening to buckle beneath her, and she was all tottery, like a baby learning to walk, as she took one tentative step and then another.

'So where's the bathroom?' He scooped her decisively into his arms and she capitulated. She could make it under her own steam but it would take for ever.

'Next floor down.' She wound her arms around his neck. He would be able to carry her more easily that way, wouldn't he? So she was simply being co-operative, wasn't she?

'What did your parents say when they saw this place?' he wanted to know as he negotiated the narrow, linoleum-covered stairs, dimly illuminated by a single, very low-wattage lightbulb.

'Not a lot.' Her fingers curled with unthinking pleasure into the thick dark hair at the nape of his neck. 'Mum had hysterics and Dad made his usual blustering noises. But when I explained that I wanted to live as cheaply as possible and plough all the profits back into the business—Mayfair premises don't come as free gifts with packets of tea, you know—then, when I was able, start saving for somewhere decent to live, they shut up. They know I do my own thing. Dad offered to buy me the lease on something very refined out Hampstead way.'

'Which you refused?' he queried drily.

'Of course. I make it on my own, or not at all.'

'Stubborn baggage!'

But there'd been a hint of a smile in his voice, a hint of approval. And that made her feel cosy, although it shouldn't. But before she had time to mourn her shortcomings, the catastrophic effect he had on her, he had pushed open the bathroom door, pulled the light switch and set her down gently in the centre of the floor.

'I'll be right outside. Shout if you need me. Don't hesitate; I'm unshockable.' The wry curve of his mouth sent her pulses skittering and she knew she would willingly drown in the deep blue ocean of his eyes. She caught her breath. She didn't need this; she couldn't handle it; she shouldn't have to try! She was going to have to make him leave, somehow.

Relief washed through her as he closed the door behind him and she clung weakly to the washbasin, hating herself. How could she love someone who belonged to someone else? And how could she love someone who resorted to cold-blooded blackmail?

So she would make herself stop loving him. Force the madness out of her system. How, she didn't quite know, but she'd do it!

She used the lavatory and held her hands under cold running water, trying to rediscover her old decisive self—the self who had always known what she was doing, where she was going, the career-orientated lady who'd had little time for the male sex and no time at all for the folly of falling in love.

She stared at her washed-out reflection in the small, functional mirror above the basin, willing some sense into her head. If she'd thought to bring her washbag and a towel she could really have freshened up and maybe felt more capable, more decisive.

'Are you all right?' Gideon stood in the doorway, big and dark and frowning.

She frowned right back. Was she to have no privacy at all? She didn't need him around when she was so desperately trying to fall out of love with him!

'I want to clean my teeth.' She knew she sounded like a three-year-old in a sulk, but didn't care. The situation was swamping her, scraping her nerves.

'Good idea. What's stopping you?'

'Fetching my washbag from my room. Three people share this bathroom. We don't leave stuff around and we clean up after ourselves. Otherwise sharing would be unbearable,' she said, tight-lipped.

Why couldn't he have left well alone, stayed home with his reluctant bride? Why couldn't he have known she had too much integrity to so much as whisper one word about what had happened to anyone? Why did he have to torment her so?

Her hands gripped the washbasin, her head flopping forward, and she could feel a band of sweat popping out across her forehead—though she knew the symptoms were due more to the discovery of her love for him than the now waning virus.

He gave her a comprehensive look then scooped her up and carried her with grim-faced determination back to her room, easing her down onto the rumpled bed.

'I'll bring a bowl of water; you can do your teeth right here. Then how about a hot drink?' he suggested, anger, irritation, whatever, all gone now as far as she could see. But she shook her head, her eyes stricken, her teeth chattering, and he made a low sound of compression and lay down beside her, wrapping his arms around her until the spasm was over and she lay still, clinging to the strength of his body.

It was so blissfully comforting to be held like this. By him. So right. It felt so right, and if she put her troublesome mind into neutral, and kept it there, she could enjoy this stolen moment of sweet contentment.

'Stay. Hold me,' she pleaded as she felt him begin to ease himself off the bed, and he went still, very still, then sighed softly, gathering her close again. She snuggled into him contentedly and opened her hand against his chest, feeling the reassuring beat of his heart as she drifted into healing sleep.

It was still dark when she woke, but cooler, much cooler, and she folded her arms right round him, instinctively cuddling closer to the source of the warmth.

The headache had gone, no aches and pains. Her whole body felt light, wonderfully purified, sensitised. And yet her mind felt as if it didn't belong to her—drugged, fuzzy, not functioning on all cylinders. Quiet. At ease. Dreaming.

He was asleep, his heartbeat slow and regular beneath her breasts, his breathing light. And it was sheer rapture to be so close to him, his arms enfolding her, keeping her safe, making her feel special, as if they belonged together.

She gave a small mewing sigh in her throat as her fingers made the discovery that his shirt had come adrift from his trousers.

The warm satin skin of his back was a temptation far too strong to be denied and her small hand moved with a dreamy feeling of inevitability beneath his shirt. She loved the feel of the hard muscle and bone, the smooth, warm skin; she adored her wonderful dream, safe within its unreality, its lack of accountability.

No one could punish you for what you did in your dreams, could they?

His formerly crisp white shirt had got all rumpled, most of the buttons undone, and that was heavenly because her cheek rested against the hair-roughened skin of his chest and, trance-like, she moved her head just slightly, careful not to wake him, just enough to put her lips against his skin, to steal a forbidden taste of him.

Soft butterfly kisses to begin with, dreamy kisses, her lips parting, barely moving at all until her neck arched without her even knowing she was doing it, giving her access to the corded column of his throat, to the vulnerable pulse-point at its base. And as she tasted his salty skin everything inside her exploded.

Deep heat surged through her body, a persistent, driving heat, a burning compulsion, a need that made her writhe against him. She felt him come instantly awake, his relaxed body tensing, his breath sucked in and tightly held.

'Alice—' He sounded tortured. 'Wake up!' He gave her a tiny shake. 'You're feverish—don't tempt me to take advantage. There's only so much a mere man can stand!'

He was trying to lighten a fraught situation, make a joke of it. But the tension in his voice was clear, his body's aroused response unmistakable. It sent her own body wild with a need she was incapable of fighting, and when he gently began to put her away from him she clung to him frantically, out of control.

'Don't go! Hold me—please hold me!' Her breath rasped in her throat as she hung onto him, her legs entwined with his. His love was what she most wanted in the world; nothing else mattered. How could it when he had become the centre of her universe?

He was here with her now, in her dream world, and there would never be another time. There was no room for anything but the two of them because the raw intensity of her need for him was all there was.

And she knew she had kept him in her wonderful dream world, because she heard his defeated groan, felt his arms move around her again, so gently, so carefully, as if she were made from the most delicate of spun glass.

He kissed her slowly, lingering softly over each delicious, delicate taste, his hands soothing her, stroking her body with reverential care, until her fevered flesh was screaming with the need for all he was withholding. She caught his head in her hands and kissed his mouth with all the wanton passion that came with frenzied desire from the wild core of a heart that was aflame with love.

He broke the kiss, holding her back against the pillow, his hands gentle on her slender shoulders, fever gripping his body now, tremors of desire rippling through his impressive frame, his breathing heavy.

She lifted her arms to him, the movement sensual, sinuous. All constraint was gone, burned to ashes in the unleashed flames of desire, and raging emotion was a tidal wave of rapturous insanity as he took her mouth again, deeply, surely, making her his possession.

And after that there was nothing but raw, driving need, the hot, swirling fires of desire, tangled naked limbs, all senses aflame as they took the whirlwind journey, soaring beyond space and time and reason to that place in heaven which was theirs alone.

CHAPTER TEN

ALICE came awake quickly, blinking her eyes, all tangled up with the big naked body of Gideon Rymer.

Her heart stopped, juddering sickeningly before racing on, her body going into shock as last night's events paraded themselves in front of her stunned brain.

What had she done? Oh, what had she done?

Hardly daring to breathe, she delicately untangled her limbs from his, her pulses pounding, her heart turning over when she saw how relaxed and beautiful he looked in sleep.

She closed her eyes on a smothered groan. What passed for her brain had been behaving despicably. She was deeply, dredgingly ashamed of herself.

Down in the quiet early-morning street she heard the whine of an electric milk float, the clank of bottles. The milkman always called at six, so that must mean she had plenty of time to creep down through the sleeping house and have her bath. She always used the bathroom first, usually pattering down at seven. She was a habitual early riser, and putting her first on the rota made sense.

Her heart in her mouth, she inched off the bed and tested her legs. Still a little shaky but they would hold her. The virus had cleared her system. She wished she could get Gideon out of her blood as quickly. He would only have to open those sleepy blue eyes, smile that slow, incomparable smile, hold out a hand to her and she would be lost, practically falling over herself to get back into bed with him.

A sob caught at her throat. She hated not being able to trust herself.

Shakily, she dragged her robe out from under the bed, stoically disregarding the wicked evidence of his discarded clothing, and slipped it on.

It was a slinky, slithery, silky thing, a recent birthday present from her mother, who never stopped trying to get her to 'make something' of herself.

Alice had thought she would never wear it, because such frivolities had no place in her life and her navy blue towelling hide-all had years of life left in it. But this summer had started so early and been so amazingly hot that she'd been forced to wear it because the other had been so stifling.

Casting a wary eye in his direction, she saw he was still asleep, and looked quickly away before her treacherous heart could betray her, surging with painful love for the heartless, deceiving brute. Purposefully gathering the things she'd need, she crept from the room and down the stairs, clinging tightly to the handrail.

Soaking in the bath was sheer bliss, with her wet hair hanging around her. But she didn't deserve the luxury, she reminded herself sharply. She deserved to be boiled in oil for what she had done.

So maybe Gideon Rymer slept around when the opportunity was so blatantly offered. So maybe his future wife had been having a furtive affair with the man she really loved. It still didn't excuse her own unforgivable behaviour.

If she hadn't fallen in love for the first time in her life it would never have happened. And what if she was pregnant?

The sudden shock of that terrifying thought brought her upright in a shower of water droplets, clutching onto the sides of the bath for dear life.

It was perfectly possible. Their lovemaking had been so spontaneous, so inevitably ecstatic. There had been no time for thought.

And she couldn't heap the blame on him. He, at least, had shown some decency last night, she reminded herself as she roughly towelled herself dry, rinsed off her hair and dragged a comb punishingly through the tangle.

Twice he'd tried to take himself back to the armchair and twice she'd pleaded with him to stay, sensing his reservations as he'd kissed her so gently, soothing her, probably trying to lull her back to sleep and so solve the problem!

But no—oh, no! That hadn't been enough for her, had it? Blood raged to her cheeks at the shameful memory. She'd practically ravaged him, an invitation no red-blooded male could have been expected to turn down. She glared at her hot little face in the mirror and hated herself.

Then she caught her passion-bruised lower lip between her teeth. She had to calm down. Slinging insults at herself, no matter how richly deserved, would get her nowhere. And going back up to her room before she'd worked out exactly what to do, what to say to convince him that she never wanted to see him again, would probably get her somewhere. Back into bed. With him.

He had enjoyed their frenzied lovemaking as much as she had. He hadn't been able to believe his luck. He would probably look at her with those wickedly smiling eyes, pop her number in his little black book and suggest he visit from time to time—provided, of course, that it was all kept deeply secret, very discreet, with nothing said or done to cause trouble with his wife.

And, knowing her miserable track record where he was concerned, she would probably end up as his mistress. Loving him, loathing herself, unable to cast off his spell.

So she had to return to that room fully armed, protected with something that would put him off her for life.

But what? Her brow wrinkled with concentration as she tied the narrow belt of the robe, wishing now that she'd taken the time to fish the old towelling thing out of the cupboard, where she'd tidied it away until the cooler weather returned.

This bright red thing flowed over each and every one of her curves, making her look positively voluptuous. But it did give her an idea. An excellent idea. Provided she could carry it off.

But she had to; there were no two ways about it. He had to be the one to walk away because she didn't trust herself to stick to her resolve never to have anything to do with him again. She loved him so much it hurt, and he could be so very persuasive.

She gathered her bits and pieces together and got herself back up the stairs. She had to make it work. If she didn't she would be damned for ever in her own eyes. She would become the type of woman she despised more than any other. The type who played around with married men. She couldn't do that to herself.

She pushed on the door to her room and saw he was awake. More than awake. Already dressed in his crumpled clothes, the shirt unbuttoned, dark stubble decorating his strong jaw. She slapped an insincere smile on her face and made herself look away from the long, approving sweep of his sexy blue eyes.

'You look fantastic, Alice. You're obviously feeling much better.'

'Heaps. A bit wobbly in the knee department, but otherwise fine.' She didn't look at him; she didn't dare. He could tempt her into betraying herself again far too easily.

She fished a clean towel out of a drawer and a fresh bar of soap and tossed them at him.

'You can use my seven o'clock slot in the bathroom, but if you want to clean your teeth you're going to have to share my brush. I don't have a spare, I'm afraid.' She had scrabbled and scrabbled, looking for one, and the normally neat contents of the drawer were in a heap. She stared at the untidy mess with consternation.

Her life, like this drawer, had become an utter mess. Chaos. And she didn't know how she was going to be tough enough to tidy it up again. It was a point rammed shamingly home when her whole body flamed and melted responsively as he told her softly, 'I'll share anything of yours, any time, sweetheart.'

She wanted to put her fingers in her ears to block out that beguiling voice, the invitation to go to his arms. But she couldn't. She had to endure, to fight back. So she made a start, drawling, 'If you don't go now the bathroom won't be free until after nine. I'll put the kettle on for tea.'

She knew he was giving her a long, considering look. She could feel it prickling down the length of her spine. It made her want to scream with physical aggravation. Biting her lip, she began to tidy the drawer methodically, and only stopped the mindless activity when she heard the door close behind him.

Then she sagged against the chest. She knew this was going to be the most difficult thing she had ever had to do in the whole of her life. She was going to have to send the man she loved away with the indelible impression that he'd bedded a hard-as-nails slut. The type of immoral harpie that any man in his right mind would run a mile from.

Her fingers went to her temples, pressing, as if she could still the hectic race of blood through her veins. She was going to have to be tough, and strong, and think about the consequences some other time.

Consequences like his being so disgusted with her he'd put in a bad word whenever he could and harm her business. Like possibly having his child and never telling him, being a one-parent family...

But not now. Later. She would think about it later. Right now she had to concentrate all her mental energies on making him walk away from her, never wanting to set eyes on her again.

She swung away from the chest and put the kettle on the gas ring, got mugs and the teapot ready and opened the fridge.

And that was almost her undoing, because it was packed with goodies. Butter, eggs, milk, a cold roast chicken and a bulging bag of fresh fruit. Not to mention gallons of tempting juices and the crusty loaf she'd discovered in the bread bin. And how could she ever forget his offering of flowers, something to add beauty to her tatty surroundings?

Tears washed her eyes, flooded her heart. Most men would have contacted a relative and then run a mile on finding a sweaty, unappetising female sprawled out on her sickbed. Many others would have simply run.

But he had stayed, caring for her beautifully, calling in his own doctor, stocking up on wholesome foods to tempt a recuperating appetite and bringing her flowers to delight her eyes. She had to admit that no one on earth could have looked after her with more care, good humour and consideration. And no one on this earth could have made love to her more beautifully...

She slapped that treacherous thought away, found her tissues, mopped her eyes, then hunted down the brightest lipstick she owned and plastered it on.

She decided she looked like a clown: dark rings round her eyes, her pallor accentuated by the glossy bright lipstick and the flamboyant robe. But all in a good cause. She made the tea and it was poured and waiting when Gideon came back into the room.

He hadn't been able to shave, of course, but his tanned skin looked fresh and clear, good enough to eat, and there was a lambent look in his fantastic eyes that wasn't there because he wanted to get his hands on his mug of tea.

He wanted to get his hands on her!

She sat down quickly. Her legs had given way at

last. She didn't know how she'd find the strength of mind to send him away.

'Alice…' He perched on the edge of the table, because there was only one dining chair and she had just collapsed onto it. And she wished he had a squeaky voice instead of rough, dark velvet that reached out to caress her, made her toes curl, her blood surge hotly, sweetly through her veins.

She didn't look at him but stared at the wall, at the square of florid wallpaper that was brighter than the rest where a previous tenant must have hung a picture.

'I came because we had to talk. You must have known I would, after you walked out and refused to wait. But you were in no state to take anything in. And now—'

'Who the heck wants to talk?' She made herself look at him then, narrowing her eyes—partly to hide her anguished expression and partly because she couldn't see him too clearly without her glasses and had to squint. She needed to see his feelings on his face, so she could judge when she'd gone far enough to convince him. 'Chewing things over is so boring, don't you think?'

She did her best to give him a sultry smile and knew she'd failed, produced only a grimace of pain. So she laved her full lower lip with the tip of her tongue—something, so she had heard, that was a very sultry thing to do. She saw his eyes narrow. 'So we made love. So what?' She wouldn't let her voice wobble and betray her. She would *not*! 'It was fun, and lovely, and—'

'Alice!' There was a rough edge of warning in his

voice. She squinted a little bit more and could clearly see that he was angry, but incredulous too.

That wasn't quite good enough. Disgust was what she was aiming for, something to put him off her for life. Her heart pumping, she flicked him a teasing smile, and if she'd been a smoker this was the time she would have lit up, blowing a lazy plume in his direction through her pouting, painted lips.

Instead, she crossed her legs with a swish of silk, leaned back in the chair so that the edges of her robe came apart and forced herself not to weep wild tears as she told him, 'But, as I was trying to warn you, I have a low boredom threshold when it comes to men. After the thrill of the first time—well, you know how it is. Off after the next!'

'You make it sound as if your life's full of one-night stands. So, how many men, Alice?'

He was watching her carefully, too carefully for her liking. He was plainly having trouble with her new persona. She felt sick. But smiled archly.

'I guess that could be classed as a leading question, Mr Rymer. Let's just say a number, and leave it at that.'

'So...' His eyes had narrowed to dark slits. 'If you're so all-fired promiscuous, how come it was you who called a halt when things started to get out of hand that night back at Rymer?'

Oh, God, she'd been digging herself a hole and hadn't seen it until she'd fallen right in! She felt as if mice were skittering around in her brain—mice with very heavy, very hot feet. Lots and lots of them.

'Oh, that,' she managed at last, hoping he wouldn't put his own interpretation on the lengthy pause. She pushed her hair languidly off her face. 'I was there on business. I don't mix business with pleasure. I thought you understood that. But last night, now, was different. My assistant's handling your commission now, which leaves me out of it. Free to indulge.'

'I don't believe I'm hearing this!' He was off the table, hauling her to her feet, a heartbeat away from shaking her head off her shoulders.

With him this close, his lean hands gripping her arms, her resolve began to slither away, all her self-respect going with it. She wanted to tell him she'd been lying; she wanted to confess her love...

She couldn't! She wouldn't!

'Believe it, big boy!' She tipped back her head, letting her eyes wander over his harsh features. She sounded like a very bad film, but all she was doing was fighting for her self-respect.

He wouldn't give a fig for her self-respect.

He would toss it aside with much amusement. When weighed against the gratification of his deeply sensual nature, a little thing like how she viewed herself would be of negligible interest. He would sweep all her protestations aside and get her back to bed with no trouble at all, make sure she kept her mouth firmly shut, and drop by for more of the same whenever he felt the need.

The thought of becoming his sex slave horrified her. Yet she loved him so much it could easily happen. She had to keep up her act. She poked a playful finger at the hard wall of his chest.

'As I've said, I get bored very easily. I guess that's why I've never wanted a regular boyfriend, marriage—all that sort of stuff. But if you're really in-

terested in having fun now and again, after you're
married, I guess I could squeeze you in.'

She tipped her head consideringly, ignoring the
way his eyes had gone black with fury and something
else she couldn't quite name, and went for the *coup
de grâce*. 'Mind you, it would cost you.'

And she watched his face go completely blank, as
if he'd never had an emotion worth speaking of in
the whole of his life. His hands dropped, as if she
contaminated him. And then she watched him walk
out of her life.

And wanted to die.

'Well, that's sorted, thank the Lord!' Rachel came
into the front office from the street, her round face
flushed and smiling and sprinkled with freckles. 'The
bride wants white flowers only; the florist suggested
lilies. The bride said they reminded her of funerals
and what about orange blossom, and the florist said—
Well…' She grinned, dropping her folder neatly into
a filing cabinet. 'You know how it goes!'

Alice did know. Not that she'd done any hands-on
work lately. She'd left all that to her assistant while
she'd sat here in the office pushing paperwork around;
meanwhile outside the pavements were shimmering
with heat and life was going on for other people.

'As long as everyone's satisfied,' she said, an edge
to her voice. She was thinking of lilies. They didn't
remind her of funerals, but of life, of love, of Gideon.
Of all that she wanted and could never have.

'Look, boss.' Rachel was standing in front of the
glass-topped desk now, her hands planted on her
pleasantly plump hips. 'Tell me to mind my own busi-

ness, if you like, but why don't you take a holiday?
Go somewhere nice, or just back to your parents' for
a proper rest. You've been back at work for a week
now and you still look washed out. That bug obviously took a lot out of you.'

Not the bug. No virus could have affected her as
Gideon had done. And her manner of getting rid of
him, once and for all, still made her feel like a worm.
The lowest of the lowlife.

Her fingers clenched around her pen and the point
stabbed a hole in an invoice. Almost frenziedly she
smoothed down the paper, then tossed her pen aside
and leaned back with a dredging sigh. Once a thing
was spoiled, broken, it could never be put right again.

She smiled wanly at Rachel. 'I'm fine.'

'No, you're not.' Her assistant was adamant. 'And
I can manage; you know I can. And if I get swamped
with paperwork I'll hire a temp. The business can
stand it.'

Yes, the business could stand it. Big fat cheques
and commissions were rolling in. Where once this
would have filled her with the pride of achievement,
all she could feel now was a grey lack of interest.

Rachel was managing magnificently, and with a
secretary to do the office work she, Alice, wouldn't
be missed. Her business, her special, precious baby,
would go on growing and flourishing without her. She
was surplus to requirements and, strangely, she didn't
care.

She had lost all that up-and-at-'em enthusiasm, all
that drive, her need to succeed and prove she could
stand on her own.

All she cared about was Gideon. He was all she

could think about now. She had even lost interest in saving hard for a decent home. She would stay where she was. Her unlovely bedsit was full of memories now—some of them bad, very bad, but it was too early to let them go.

So she could splurge what was left of her savings on an exotic cruise, she supposed, with no enthusiasm at all.

She certainly couldn't face going home to the stockbroker belt and listening to her mother wittering on about it being time she settled down, found herself a husband and started a family before it was too late. Listening to her going on about how well her sisters had done for themselves, suffering the bluff heartiness of her father, seeing the blunt incomprehension in his eyes as he wondered how this cuckoo had managed to arrive in the nest.

No, she loved her family to pieces, but she needed to be back to full strength, totally calm and resigned to what she had made of her life before she could be in their company for more than a minute.

'I'll think about taking a break,' she promised Rachel.

But she didn't. The only useful thought she had was when she opened the office the following morning and flipped through the post.

Gideon's marriage was still going ahead. There had been no cancellation and all the arrangements were well in hand. Had poor Janet felt this draining, helpless heartbreak when she'd said goodbye to the man she loved and turned her face firmly towards her duty?

Alice's own aching heart went out to her. Guilt rose

up to swamp her. She had had an affair—if that tempestuous, strangely inevitable coming together could be called that—with the man the poor girl was somehow being forced to marry. And the fact that Gideon didn't love Janet, and she didn't love him, did nothing to mitigate the guilt and shame of it.

Somehow she had to do something for her. Her own life was chaos, misery, but Janet's needn't be that way.

The marriage had to be stopped.

And as for Gideon—well, he didn't love Janet and he would survive the loss of the property she would have brought to the marriage. He'd find some other suitable woman to bear his children with no trouble at all. Janet wouldn't survive so easily; the loss of love was almost impossible to bear.

She wouldn't stand by and see Janet throw love away.

When Rachel came in, moments later, Alice said, 'Right. As of tomorrow you're on your own. I'll take that break. Just for a few days.'

She was going to have to forget her vow that she would never, unless it was completely unavoidable—like death and taxes and televised cricket—allow herself to set eyes on Gideon again.

She was going to Rymer to ask him to release Janet.

Whatever it cost her in heartbreak, she was going to help. Gideon owed Janet an explanation.

CHAPTER ELEVEN

RYMER COURT. Looking as lovely as it had done when Alice had first set eyes on it on the last day of her innocence. She'd been bright and perky then, all fired up to do a job, blissfully ignorant of what was about to happen.

How long ago it seemed, and yet it wasn't, not when measured in weeks and days. No time at all for her life to have changed out of all recognition.

But it seemed like for ever. Love had taken over her life, making everything else seem worthless by comparison.

And love was out of her reach.

Cutting the engine, she stared through the windscreen. The house seemed strangely lifeless. In a few short weeks' time, if Gideon had his way, it would be full of men in morning suits and ladies in summery dresses, wearing very high heels and very big hats. The thought made her feel ill.

Not if she could help it! Not if she did the right thing.

And it would be right, wouldn't it? To ask Gideon to stop the wedding, plead if necessary? Ever since she'd decided on this course of action she'd gone over and over everything, convincing herself of her duty.

Janet and Will were in love. That was a fact.

Gideon was making it impossible for Janet to call the whole thing off and marry Will. That was a fact.

164

And the implication thrown up by that was blackmail—some hold he had over the wretched girl. And, as Janet had admitted, property was involved. That had to mean the Manor and its land.

Gideon wasn't in love with Janet. He wanted a nice, safe little wife, one who would be loyal, undemanding, a good breeder and a dedicated organiser of his creature comforts—as unlike his long-lost mother as it was possible to be. Moreover, a wife who would pretend not to notice those of his sexual misdemeanours he was unlucky enough to be found out in.

But he wasn't all bad, so surely he would listen? Everyone around him adored him. And a man didn't get that kind of love and loyalty if he was a total creep.

Oh, he had charm in barrow-loads, fantastic looks, brains and money, and sex appeal that could hit a poor, unsuspecting girl like a sledgehammer. But there was something else about the man, something deeper, something bewitchingly compelling that pulled people's strings whether they wanted them pulled or not.

He had certainly pulled hers, she reflected miserably, tweaked them so hard that she had, for a brief time, lost all moral values, had been unable to keep control of her emotions.

She had allowed them to run riot, landing her in havoc, and the only thing she could do to make amends was persuade him to release Janet. Appeal to his better nature.

And he *did* have a better nature, she reminded herself, fearing the temptation to turn tail and run would get the better of her. Look at the way he'd cared for her when she'd been ill.

So sitting here, trying to pluck up courage, wasn't going to achieve anything, she told herself, willing the over-active butterflies in her stomach to settle down, take a rest, give her a break.

He had carried away a rotten impression of her, one she had deliberately given him, so he wasn't likely to be overjoyed to see her. But he wouldn't throttle her and throw her in the bushes, would he? He was far too civilised.

It was the look of contempt in his eyes she dreaded. She had drawn him a picture of a female possessed of much the same sexual morals as he himself. He hadn't liked the look of it. A case of the old double standards, of course.

Sighing, she left the car and set off for the rear of the house in search of Dona. She found her in the kitchen, listlessly stirring something in a bowl. 'Listless' wasn't a word she associated with the bubbly half-Italian girl, and when Alice said her name it came out like a question.

'Alice!' Astonishingly, a look of pure joy flooded the lovely face, and she abandoned the bowl, her arms outstretched as she bounded over the floor to give Alice a quick hug. 'Thank heavens you've come!'

'Well. Yes.' What could she say to such an effusive greeting? And then the penny dropped. It could only be because of the wedding arrangements.

Janet was resigned to her fate, and wouldn't argue or make a fuss over anything because she didn't care, and Gwen would fall in with any old plan. So maybe the unknown quantity, stepmother Rose, had started meddling on her return from Canada—altering this, changing that, generally making life difficult.

Alice didn't know, and didn't want to hang around to find out. If she had her way there would be no wedding. And she didn't want to see any of the others—especially not Janet—until she'd talked to Gideon.

'I don't have much time,' she prevaricated. 'I need to see Gideon. Where is he? In his study?'

'He's not here.'

'Oh, no!' Alice wailed. She should have telephoned ahead, saved herself a wasted journey, avoided all this angst. Now she would have to go through all this again, psyching herself up to the point where she felt able to face him.

'He went over to the Manor House early this morning,' Dona commented idly, all straight-faced, but her big brown eyes dancing with mischief. 'On foot. If you follow you should meet him on his way back. And you will put a smile on his face! He's been like a black thundercloud all week—working, working all the time, even though he's supposed to be taking a vacation. And a smile—getting a smile from him has been impossible!'

'I'll try and find him.' Alice scurried out. She'd been right. The wedding arrangements were in a tangle. Why else should he be like a thundercloud? He probably found the whole thing deeply irritating and couldn't bring himself to contact her and tell her to come and sort it out.

Which didn't augur well for her project, did it? Why would he listen to a word she said when he couldn't bring himself to pick up the phone and demand she sort out the mess that was brewing here? And as for putting a smile on his face—pigs might fly!

But she had got herself here and she had to try. She owed it to Janet. And when he knew that his supposedly wishy-washy, compliant fiancée had had a passionate affair with another man, fallen fathoms-deep in love with him, he would change his mind about the marriage.

Her behaviour would remind him too much of his mother's, and he wouldn't countenance that.

And Janet would be free to be with the man she loved. Her job would be done. She would have made amends.

Her feet dragged as she followed the track through the belt of trees. She put it down to the heat, but knew she'd been lying to herself when Gideon appeared and her heart stopped beating and her blood turned to ice.

'Thundercloud' had been the wrong word to describe him. His features looked as if they'd been carved from granite by a sculptor with a grudge against the human race. There was no expression at all except the merest flicker of surprise—or was it shock?—in those narrowed, flinty eyes.

'What do you want?' His voice was hard and cool and she mourned the warmth, the effortless charm, the shattering way he had of smiling, as if she were the most special woman in the world. It made her feel as if the sun had gone in on her life.

But, as this was exactly what she'd expected, what she had mentally prepared herself to meet, she found her voice and told him, 'I want to talk to you.'

'And I don't want to listen.' He made to brush past

her, but the track was narrow and she grabbed her courage in both hands and blocked him.

Cold eyes raked her, flicking from her head to her feet and back again in icy contempt. Her heart lurched with an indescribable pain. He was looking at her as if she were something disgusting he'd found on the bottom of his shoes, and, while she wasn't in her prim business gear, but was wearing an old pair of denim cut-offs with a white T-shirt and sandals, her hair neatly braided, she wasn't dressed as a scarlet woman either—as she had been at the time of their last traumatic encounter.

But she had earned his contempt, had earned it deliberately, she reminded herself. And she hadn't come here expecting to be welcomed, had she? She wasn't here on her own account.

'I don't want to talk about me—us—' She floundered there, hating the way her face crawled with hot colour. The last thing she'd meant to do was remind him. But she picked herself up again and added firmly, before he told her to go away and stop contaminating his land, 'I want to talk about Janet. I guess you won't want to hear that either. But it's important. I wouldn't have come here if it weren't.'

No, he wouldn't want to hear that the docile little heiress he'd picked up for himself was capable of deep passion for another man. But she had to get through to him. And he wouldn't be hurt—or only in the pride and avarice department. He'd soon get over that.

'What about her?'

At least she thought she'd detected a flicker of interest there. And as he began to walk back towards the house he didn't object to her tagging along—well, not to the extent of telling her to get lost.

'If you're worried about your fee, forget it,' he added on a snap of impatience. 'You'll get every penny. I'll foot the printer's bill for the alterations to the invitations, so you won't lose any of your precious profit. That's why you came, isn't it? And Rose altered the guest list so you've been saved that hassle.'

He pushed further ahead of her on the track, and she stared at his broad back and wondered what he was talking about. Why this sudden stress on the financial side of things? Why had the guest list and invitations been changed? And why hadn't Hearts and Flowers been informed?

She had to run to catch up with him, and her breath was coming in agitated puffs as she emerged behind him onto the sweeping lawns and flowerbeds surrounding the secluded swing seat.

'I don't know what you're talking about,' she gasped, her breasts heaving beneath the soft white fabric of her T-shirt and a smothered sob catching at her throat.

He gave her a bored, withering look and drawled, 'You still here?' He hooked his thumbs into the pockets of the faded denims he was wearing with a sleeveless, washed-out blue cotton shirt. He rocked back on the heels of his scuffed leather boots, one black brow raised in query, as if waiting for her to explain why she hadn't disappeared on her broom-stick.

'I don't know what you're talking about,' she repeated, fighting tears. She had earned his contempt but didn't know how to handle it. It hurt so much it was tearing her apart. 'If there was something wrong with the invitations, I should have been told,' she insisted, in a voice choked with misery.

'Ah.' His mouth compressed with irritation. 'Jan said she'd let you know, but obviously she didn't.' He lifted his shoulders in a shrug that looked contrived. 'I contacted the printer to make the alterations to avoid having to go through you. Jan said she'd phone and let you know what was happening. The excitement must have pushed it out of her head.'

His mouth went tight, silver fury burning in his eyes. 'I'm quite sure you understand why I didn't want further contact with you.'

The savagery of his eyes, the words he'd said, the whiplash of his voice defeated her. Her head drooped forward in mute acknowledgement. Of course she understood.

And she had failed in what she'd come here to do. She hadn't pleaded with him to release Janet. She couldn't. Not now. His bitter contempt was something she was incapable of dealing with. She had made herself believe she could, but it was beyond her; she couldn't bear another second of this torture.

His voice lashed her again. 'To put the record straight, I'll tell you what Jan should have informed you of over a week ago. The arrangements are going ahead as planned, apart from the guest list and invitations, which you now know about. With one major difference. Will Gaunt is to be the bride-groom.'

His voice washed over her in icy waves, seeming to come from a great distance away. The words didn't make sense at first, but when they did she sat down heavily on the padded seat, her legs giving way.

'Janet told you about Will?' Her big grey eyes

stared at him, unblinking behind her owly glasses. She had put herself through this pain and humiliation for nothing. Janet had found the courage to tell him she wouldn't be coerced into marriage.

'Two seconds after I'd told her our marriage couldn't go ahead,' he confirmed curtly. 'I'd wanted to speak to her before she got embroiled with that designer, but the barn fire put a stop to that. I told her that our comfortable, convenient arrangement had to be cancelled because I'd done what I'd always sworn I wouldn't. I'd fallen in love.

'It didn't matter that she was beautiful, a very determined career woman and a mass of hang-ups. I just wanted her and loved her and was sure I could make her love me.' His mouth curled with self-contempt and his eyes were hard. 'But she did a bunk. She'd promised to wait, but she didn't.

'After I settled things down here, I followed her. I thought she'd had an attack of conscience, or one of those self-doubts she was ridiculously prey to, and couldn't believe that what there was between us was in any way special. I found her, all right, and came away with a nasty dose of reality.' His sarcasm ripped through her like a rusty knife. 'I'd like you off my premises. But don't twist an ankle in the rush; I couldn't bring myself to pick you up this time.'

She watched him stride away across the grass, his shoulders high and wide and hard. She wrapped her arms around her body, shivering in the sunlight. He couldn't have made his hatred plainer.

And yet—

He had said he loved her. He had released Janet

from her promise because he had finally fallen in love. With her!

Was she stupid, or what?

Running across the grass as if an Olympic Gold were at stake, she was brought to a breathless halt by a strident, 'Hey! You!' And she blinked around her and saw Tossie marching towards her through the rose garden, a spray-can held like a weapon in her hands.

'What have you done to him now?' the gorgeous gardener wanted to know, her glare ferocious. 'Dona said you were here and we thought everything would be all right. But he's just marched past me looking as if he'd like to pull the whole world down round his ears.

'And don't tell me it's nothing to do with you, 'cos I know different. Jan told us. He's in love with you. And when he came back after visiting you he was in a foul mood. Nobody dared speak to him about it, except Rose, and she came away looking as if she'd had several large fleas shoved in her ears! And now his mood's even fouler. So it's down to you. What's the matter? Isn't he good enough for you?'

Alice gave her what she hoped passed for a reassuring smile, keeping a wary eye on the spray-can at the same time. Tossie was a big girl, and the way she was holding it looked decidedly menacing.

'Just a misunderstanding,' she said quickly. 'Which way did he go?'

'Up there.' Tossie, not taking her eyes from Alice, jerked her head at the steps up to the terrace. 'And if you hurt him one more time I'll—'

'I won't,' Alice promised, lifting her shoulders

helplessly. What she had thought—assumed—the lengths she had gone to to make him stay away from her didn't matter now. It had to be put behind her.

Her face set, she flew up the steps to the terrace. What if Gideon had really washed his hands of her? Fallen out of love as quickly as he'd fallen in?

His love. Such an infinitely precious thing. She hadn't known she had it. What if she'd destroyed it?

It didn't bear thinking about.

He wasn't in the sitting room so she headed straight for his study and he was there, sitting in the swivel chair behind his desk, looking through the window that overlooked the drive with his back to her—probably waiting to make sure she got in her car and drove away, out of his life.

He hadn't heard her push the door open and she stood on the threshold, hardly able to breathe. Had she left it far too late to put things right?

She knew she hadn't made a sound and yet she saw the muscles of his wide shoulders clench, as if he'd sensed her presence in the room. Then the chair swivelled round, and just in that one moment she saw her own anguish mirrored in his eyes before they blanked out and he stated harshly, 'I asked you to leave.'

'Yes, I know. But I'm not going.' She had seen the pain in his eyes; she hadn't imagined it. And that gave her the courage to march across the room and look him straight in the eye. 'You love me. And I love you. Forget that stuff I said. I love you.'

'Really? I wonder when that happened?' he drawled, his eyes like chips of ice. But his hands were gripping the arms of the chair until the knuckles showed white.

He wasn't as coldly collected as he was pretending to be, and she was able to ignore his insulting tone when he said, 'About the same time you learned I wouldn't be marrying Jan? Fancied a luxurious pad in the country, did you? Make a change from that grot-hole you live in. Money too. Plenty of it—all without having to work your socks off to earn it. Enough there to keep the sexual boredom at bay? For a month or two? Or longer? A whole year, at a pinch?'

She had heard enough. She launched herself into his lap, knocking the air from his lungs, and muttered, 'I am not your mother!' She smothered his mouth with hers and kissed him until he kissed her back, and she didn't know who had driven who wild. Her head was spinning so dizzily that when they drew apart for the necessity of air she spluttered, 'Now tell me you don't want me!'

'Bitch!' His voice was low, tight, an explosion waiting to happen, but his hands still held her as if he'd never let go, and she leaned forward and ran the tip of her tongue over his parted lips and felt response rocket through him. She was getting the hang of seducing him, loving it.

'I knew you'd say that,' she told him sagely. 'Because you still believe I get through a dozen men a month.'

'And don't you?' His voice was raw, his eyes anguished as they held hers.

'I was lying,' she confessed, loving him so much it hurt. 'There was only one before you, and that was years ago and a bit of a farce, so it doesn't count. I thought I was in love with him—can you imagine? I didn't know the meaning of the word.' She snuggled deeper into his lap, keeping her fingers crossed that he wouldn't tip her off and throw her out of the window.

He seemed to be holding his breath as she went on, 'You see, I'd fallen in love with you and knew I shouldn't have. And we made love, and we shouldn't have done that either. I felt guilty as hell because you were marrying Janet, and I knew I had to say something really bad about myself to put you off me for life—or I'd end up being a married man's bit on the side, and I couldn't let myself do that.'

'Oh, Alice!' There was a catch in his deep, husky voice. 'You couldn't have come up with a better way of sending me packing if you'd employed a team of expert psychologists! In those few words you made yourself a grotesque caricature of everything I'd been brought up to believe my mother was! Just a few words—enough to saddle me with all my father's black bitterness. If I'd been thinking straight I'd have seen through your lies.' He dragged in a shuddering breath. 'How could I have believed you were a scarlet woman in prim little wedding organiser's clothing?'

He seemed shattered—more by what he had learned about himself than by her own confession. Her fingers were gently stroking the naked, hair-roughened skin of his arms, and she felt the steely muscles tense and flex. And although he still wasn't saying anything to relieve her fears she hoped and prayed that he was going to forgive her.

To help him see the whole picture, she told him

breathily, 'I came here today to ask you not to force poor Janet to marry you—because of Will. I'd found out she was in love with him, and—'

'What gave you that idea? Am I so repulsive that I'd have to force a woman to marry me?'

He jerked upright so suddenly she had to wrap both arms around his neck to prevent an undignified descent to the floor. She put her nose an inch from his and held his eyes intently.

'We're not going to get ourselves all tangled over this. True, I didn't like the idea of blackmail. But I forgave you. I tried to tell myself I couldn't love a man who stooped that low, but it didn't make any difference. You can't love to order, can you? When I first came here—'

'Very prim and proper. A Ms with a mission,' he drawled softly, making her frown.

'Don't interrupt.' Was he trying to ease her away from the subject of blackmail? She'd told him she'd already forgiven him. And why had he softened? Did he accept that she'd been lying? Did he believe she loved him? 'I dare say you had your reasons—not very laudable ones—but you didn't carry out your threat to marry her.'

'Uh-huh.' He looked very relaxed now. 'So I have to use threats now, do I, to get a woman?' His arms had tightened around her, and the end of his handsome nose was closer than it had been, so she knew they'd forgiven each other, but he wasn't going to wriggle out of a well-deserved lecture by—

She removed one hand from her stranglehold around his neck to slap away the fingers that were inching beneath the hem of her T-shirt. 'Stop that! I'm talking.'

Her eyes went wide, mesmerised by the slumberous, sexy look in his, and she cleared her throat and said quickly, 'Where was I? Yes, Janet. I could tell she was miserable about something as soon as I arrived, but I didn't know what until I found her that evening, over at the Manor with Will. She begged me not to say anything to you, and then I met you on the way back. You'd been really miffy with me, one way and another—'

'Because I was growing too attracted to you, fascinated by you. I kissed you—I thought I was being friendly, demonstrating that you were fanciable, a beautiful woman who shouldn't dress like a battle-axe—and then I felt you respond and had to back off quickly. If I'd held you a moment longer things would have got well and truly out of hand.

'And then, when you appeared for dinner that evening, you looked so heart-stoppingly beautiful and I knew I was in danger of getting in deeper than was wise. So I told you to finish up here and get out. It was the only thing I could do. I was going to marry Jan. The sooner you were gone, the less temptation I'd have to endure. And then, when we met up that night, you'd hurt your ankle—'

'I only pretended I had, to stop you going to collect Janet and finding out what was going on. She was in a terrible state.'

'And so were we,' he recalled, his smile wicked, 'when we got back to your room and started verbally lashing each other and ended up in each other's arms. That was when I gave up the fight and knew I couldn't marry Jan. Knew I was in love with you and wanted you with me always.'

'But I didn't know that and neither did she,' she pointed out earnestly. 'She came to my room early the next morning, and I felt so ashamed of myself. She told me then that she was in love with Will but had to marry you. There were compelling reasons, she said. She didn't want to talk about it, but admitted that property was involved. I knew there was no way she would marry you, loving Will, unless she didn't dare refuse.'

'Idiot!' He plucked her glasses off her nose and dropped them on the desk. He kissed her until she was sobbing for breath and then said raggedly, 'This is getting out of hand. Again.' His eyes were wry as he traced the trembling outline of her passion-bruised lips with his finger then put both hands on her shoulders, stopping her launching herself at him again.

'Let's get one thing clear, before we find somewhere more comfortable where you can tell me just how much you love me. I didn't threaten Jan, or force her into agreeing to marry me. I suggested it. Bear in mind my thought processes.' He gave her a crooked grin.

'At the time the idea of falling in love, putting myself in the position of having my future happiness dependent on another person, was not on my agenda. I hadn't met you, didn't know how ideas could change overnight. So I suggested marriage. It seemed a good idea then. We'd known each other for years, liked and respected each other, and now I'd come back to Rymer permanently and begun to look to the future. In terms of a family.

'I told her I didn't think much of the state of being "in love". My father had been besotted with my mother and her behaviour turned him into a bitter man. His bitterness rubbed off on me, I guess. And when I married I wanted it to be for solid, sensible reasons. Besides, I felt sorry for her and Gwen. Inherited guilt.'

'Guilt?' Alice put her head on one side, pursing her lips.

'If you look at me like that,' Gideon growled, 'I'll have to kiss you until we're both silly, and then you'll never get that blackmailing bee out of your beautiful bonnet. OK? Where were we? Guilt. Right.

'Jan's family have been at the Manor for generations. Her father, Ralph, was a gentle soul—immensely likeable but weak. His estate had been mismanaged for years, his investments had failed spectacularly and everything was going to pot. He was facing bankruptcy and in failing health when he approached my father for a loan.

'Now, Dad was a shrewd manipulator, played the stock market all his life, and it's my guess he saw the opportunity to make a killing—pay off Ralph's debts and have first call on the property should he fall behind with repayments. If I'd known what kind of deal he was setting up I'd have stopped it, warned Ralph not to touch it. But I was living in town then, and my visits to Rymer were rare and only to see Rose.

'Of course Ralph couldn't service the loan and, as I later learned, Dad called in the principal and threatened court action. I hope he was bluffing but I'll never know, because shortly after that Ralph's car hit a stone wall at speed, killing him outright, and days later Dad died from a massive stroke.

'Ralph's death was put down to an accident, but those of us who knew him wonder about that verdict. He was a careful driver; he rarely exceeded forty miles an hour. In any case—' he shrugged his broad shoulders '—Jan and her mother were left in a terrible financial situation. There was no way they could hang onto the Manor. Gwen, in particular, was distraught.

'So, because I knew them so well and felt enormous affection for them both—not to mention feeling responsible for what my father had done—I put a rescue package together. I bought the Manor and its estate, hired Will to bring it back to profitability, promised Gwen her home was hers for life and proposed to Jan. Jan accepted and Gwen was over the moon, but what I hadn't counted on was fate.

'When Jan and Will met they fell in love. If the silly girl had told me I'd have released her at once, with my blessing. I'm far too fond of her to stand in the way of her happiness. And I didn't know that Gwen had got the idea that the deal over the Manor was contingent on Jan becoming my wife.'

'So Janet thought she had to marry you, or she and Gwen would be out on the street?' Alice mused tenderly, her heart swelling to bursting point because he wasn't the avaricious villain of the piece but the hero. *Her* hero!

'Apparently,' he concurred wryly. 'When Jan told her mother that she'd fallen for Will and didn't want to go through with the wedding, Gwen got hysterical and came out with all sorts of garbage about the deal over the Manor falling through, leaving them in the you-know-what, if Jan even thought of doing anything so stupid.

'Now…' His hands captured hers and wound them around his neck. 'Where were we?' His own hands slid up beneath her T-shirt to cup her breasts, caressing and teasing until she thought she would faint. 'I remember. You said you loved me. So, convince me.'

So she did, as convincingly as she knew how, kissing him until the whole world fractured into a million glittering pieces.

Everything was going out of control, just as it should, when a loud, jubilant shriek brought them tumbling back to reality.

Tossie stood in the doorway, her lovely face beaming.

'Just checking you weren't killing each other!'

Alice, her face scarlet, tugged her T-shirt modestly back to where it should be and tried to wriggle off Gideon's lap, but he held her firmly where she was.

'We'll only get homicidal if we don't get some privacy,' he announced drily, lazily and with intent, unbraiding her long golden hair. 'Ask Dona to bring champagne and a couple of glasses. Alice and I have decided to marry.'

It was news to her, but she wasn't arguing. It was the best possible news. She loved him so much; she was the luckiest woman in the world, she decided as Tossie squealed with delight again and leapt across the room to enfold them both in a bear hug.

'Keep the news between yourself and Dona for now,' Gideon instructed. 'I'll break it over dinner tonight. Where are they all, by the way?'

'At Will's cottage.' Tossie grinned. 'Hanging frilly curtains and cleaning out the bath—making it fit for a new bride. Will won't know what's hit him, and he won't be able to find a thing when they've finished tidying up.'

'Good.' Gideon waited until Tossie was bounding to the door on her way to give Dona the good news and pass on the request for champagne and then said, 'One more thing. The garden's strictly out of bounds for the rest of the afternoon. You can stay indoors and help Dona prepare the fatted calf. Understood?'

Judging from the wicked sparkle in Tossie's big blue eyes, it obviously was, and Alice decided that being in love had made her slow on the uptake when, after a broadly grinning Dona had delivered the chilled champagne and her congratulations, Gideon swept the bottle up by its neck, grabbed the two glasses, and ushered her outside.

'I think a gentle stroll is called for, don't you, my love?'

His free hand was around her waist, his long fingers tucked beneath the waistband of her cut-offs, resting against her heated skin. A stroll round the gardens admiring the flowers obviously wasn't what he really had in mind, and it only lasted until they reached the swinging seat, whereupon he drew the champagne cork, filled the flutes with foaming bubbles and said, 'To you, my darling love. To us. To our long and happy future.'

She only managed a tiny sip because his eyes were so loving, so tender, that she wanted to shed tears of perfect happiness. But she put the glass down instead and wound her arms around his neck, pulling him down to the seat where she twined herself around him and gave herself up to the rapture of having every exposed inch of her skin covered with sinfully lingering kisses.

'Do you remember when we sat here and talked?' he murmured at last, his voice thick. 'I knew then that what I felt for you was far more than friendly interest. I don't go around kissing every female in sight, but with you I couldn't help it. It was natural. Imperative. But, like a fool, I fought what I was beginning to feel. A criminal waste.'

'Mmm,' she agreed dreamily. 'I remember. How could I ever forget? It was when I fell in love with you.'

And then they didn't talk at all, not for a very long time.

'You can't!' Mrs Rampton was shocked. 'It's bad luck for the groom to see the bride before the wedding!'

'Mum, don't fuss.' Alice turned in a swirl of ivory satin and faced her outraged parent. Arabella, Amaryllis and Angel were vying for mirror space and grumbling good-naturedly at each other, too interested in their own appearance to give a thought to the bride and her doings.

'I need to tell him something,' she explained, her huge eyes anxious beneath the gossamer-fine veil, secured by the yellow rosebuds Tossie had fashioned into a circlet.

'What?' her mother wanted to know. 'Can't it wait?'

Alice shook her head. It couldn't wait. She had

meant to keep her secret until after the ceremony, share it with him as her wedding gift. But now she knew she couldn't do that.

'It won't take a moment,' she promised gently.

Poor Mum had had to give way on so many fronts over this wedding. She'd been as proud as a peacock with a dozen tails when her ugly-duckling daughter had revealed her wedding plans. The awkward little thing had actually, and amazingly, done even better for herself than the three beauties of the family.

Then Alice had insisted on living with her future husband before the wedding, with only the servants to chaperon them—and they really didn't count—because all the responsible females had moved out of the house. Janet had moved to the cottage with her new husband, and Gwen and Rose had taken up residence at the Manor. And as for wanting to be married from the groom's home, instead of her own—why, it was unthinkable!

But Alice had had long practice in getting her own way. Her father, because his wife had said he must, had huffed and puffed a bit, but his eyes had been twinkling, admiring her single-mindedness.

She would never willingly spend a second away from Gideon for the rest of her life.

She caught up the skirts of her sensational Nico McGill gown and headed for the door, ignoring her mother's protests.

She found her beloved Gideon in the master bedroom, resplendent in morning dress, fixing his silver stock. He saw her shimmering reflection in the mirror and turned, his eyes filled with love as he walked towards her.

'I always knew you were beautiful, but this—' He spread his hands. 'Are you truly mine? Are you even real? Can I touch?'

Her sparkling eyes invited. Of course he could touch. She had suggested a quiet wedding, just close family, but he had insisted on the lot, a huge, traditional wedding, so the way she looked was all his doing. And the way her body was blossoming beneath the sculptured satin was all his doing too, as his beautiful, clever hands rediscovered the warm reality of her curvy person.

'I have something to tell you.' She had to fight to get her voice to work; his touch took all her breath away.

'That you love me?' His voice was husky too, his lips as he touched her own very warm and firm.

She shook her head. 'No. Oh! Of course I do! But it isn't that. I'd meant to tell you after the wedding, as—as, well, as my wedding gift to you.'

She was feeling very flustered, and the way his eyes had narrowed on her troubled face wasn't helping at all. But she had to tell him—tell him now. She took a deep breath. 'I'm—we're pregnant. I mean, we're having a baby. And I suddenly thought—well, that if I didn't tell you until after we were married you might think I'd only married you because—'

Her words were stopped by the pressure of his mouth on hers, his arms tight enough to crush her bones.

'Alice, my darling,' he breathed at last. 'You bring me nothing but delight!' And he would have said more, much more, but her father poked his head round the door.

'I don't want to frighten you, Alice, but your mother's having kittens. And you—son—you should be at the church right now. Or so I was told.'

'Right.' Gideon kissed her smiling lips and gently lowered her veil. 'See you at the altar, my precious. Walk carefully!'

And Alice took her father's arm, accepted her bouquet from her anxiously hovering mother, and descended the stairs to make her marriage vows to the most wonderful man in existence.

The world's bestselling romance series.

HARLEQUIN®
Presents

Seduction and Passion Guaranteed!

THE PRINCESS BRIDES

For duty, for money…for passion!

Discover a thrilling new trilogy from a rising star of Harlequin Presents®, Jane Porter!

Meet the Royals…

Chantal, Nicolette and Joelle are members of the blue-blooded Ducasse family. Step inside their sophisticated and glamorous world and watch as these beautiful princesses find they have to marry three international playboys—for duty, for money… and definitely for passion!

Don't miss

THE SULTAN'S BOUGHT BRIDE (#2418)
September 2004

THE GREEK'S ROYAL MISTRESS (#2424)
October 2004

THE ITALIAN'S VIRGIN PRINCESS (#2430)
November 2004

Pick up a Harlequin Presents® novel and you will enter a world of spine-tingling passion and provocative, tantalizing romance!

Available wherever Harlequin books are sold.

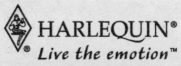

HARLEQUIN®
Live the emotion™

www.eHarlequin.com

The world's bestselling romance series.

HARLEQUIN®
Presents

Seduction and Passion Guaranteed!

We are pleased to announce
Sandra Marton's fantastic new series

In order to marry, they've got to gamble on love!

Don't miss...
KEIR O'CONNELL'S MISTRESS

Keir O'Connell knew it was time to leave Las Vegas when he became consumed with desire for a dancer. The heat of the desert must have addled his brain! He headed east and set himself up in business—but thoughts of the dancing girl wouldn't leave his head.
And then one day there she was, Cassie...

Harlequin Presents #2309
On sale March 2003

Pick up a Harlequin Presents® novel and you will enter a world of spine-tingling passion and provocative, tantalizing romance!

Available wherever Harlequin books are sold.

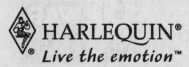

HARLEQUIN®
Live the emotion™

Visit us at www.eHarlequin.com

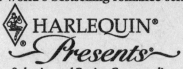

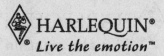

The world's bestselling romance series.

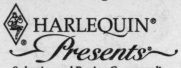

HARLEQUIN®
Presents

Seduction and Passion Guaranteed!

Your dream ticket to the vacation of a lifetime!

Why not relax and allow Harlequin Presents® to whisk you away
to stunning international locations with our new miniseries…

*Where irresistible men and sophisticated women
surrender to seduction under the golden sun.*

**Don't miss this opportunity to experience glamorous
lifestyles and exotic settings in:**

This Month:
MISTRESS OF CONVENIENCE
by Penny Jordan
on sale August 2004, #2409

Coming Next Month:
IN THE ITALIAN'S BED
by Anne Mather
on sale September 2004, #2416

Don't Miss!
THE MISTRESS WIFE
by Lynne Graham
on sale November 2004, #2428

FOREIGN AFFAIRS… A world full of passion!

Pick up a Harlequin Presents® novel and you will enter a world
of spine-tingling passion and provocative, tantalizing romance!

Available wherever Harlequin books are sold.

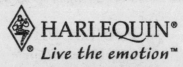

HARLEQUIN®
Live the emotion™

www.eHarlequin.com

HPFAUPD